AN ATLAS OF LOVE

Anuja Chauhan is the bestselling author of *The Zoya Factor*, *Battle for Bittora* and *Those Pricey Thakur Girls*. Popularly known as the rom-com specialist, she is the undisputed expert in writing contemporary Indian romance novels that pack in oodles of wit, punch and humour—our very own Jane Austen who understands the pulse of desi love stories.

An Atlas of Love

EDITED BY

ANUJA CHAUHAN

RUPA

First published by
Rupa Publications India Pvt. Ltd 2014
7/16, Ansari Road, Daryaganj
New Delhi 110002

Sales Centres:

Allahabad Bengaluru Chennai
Hyderabad Jaipur Kathmandu
Kolkata Mumbai

The pieces included in this anthology are works of fiction. Names, characters, places and incidents are either the product of the author's imagination or are used fictitiously and any resemblance to any actual person, living or dead, events or locales is entirely coincidental.

ISBN: 978-81-291-3000-6

First impression 2014

10 9 8 7 6 5 4 3 2 1

Contents

Introduction

WRITING IS a lonely business. The writer gets semi-horizontal someplace quiet, places the laptop on her stomach (with a pillow below it to keep things from getting too hot) and then hammers away till her mind goes blank. It's essentially an outpouring, which begs the question, well then, what about the *in*pouring? Where does all that stuff come from? The people, the plot, the little nuances?

The inpouring, of course, comes from life. From the people the writer meets, the books she reads, the experiences she has, the multiple perspectives and viewpoints on the same issue that she is privy to. From the thoughts that cross her mind because of something she saw or heard or read or felt. And it was the laalach for just such a mother lode of inpouring that got me to edit this romance anthology.

My interest was piqued when Kausalya Saptharishi from Rupa Publications told me that through the Rupa Romance Contest, I'd get to read lots of love stories, written by first-time writers from all across India—and I was on board.

Inpouring aside, there is also the fact that I'm a sucker

for love stories. Anybody's. *Everybody's.* Not just the ones with handsome heroes, feisty heroines, lashings of humour and happy endings—though I must confess that those are my favourite. I also like the not-so-happy ones, the full-on tragic ones, and the ones with the twist I never saw coming. I like them all.

Atlas of Love contains sixteen stories out of the several thousands of entries that Rupa received since we announced this contest in April 2013. There's no special significance to this number. It just happens to be the number of stories we liked (after a *lot* of agonizing and dithering and revising of lists) well enough to put into this collection.

It's called (rather grandiosely!) an 'Atlas' because it seeks to explore the many facets of love—the giggly, giddy excitement of the first crush; the mature resurgence that marks the second go at love; gay love, which demands the heavy price of crippling soul-searching and social ostracization; sadism masquerading as love; unrequited love; and the psychological aspect of obsessive self-love.

Three stories stand out for special mention. 'Phoenix Mills', which so beautifully captures the rootless randomness of our busy materialistic lives; 'Siddharth', which nails the nebulousness and confusion of long-distance relationships, and 'The Unseen Boundaries of Love', which compellingly lays bare the hypocrisies of our 'middle-class Indian values'. 'Mixed Exotica Goes to the Party' (selected as her favourite from the anthology by RJ Sayema of Purani Jeans, Radio Mirchi 98.3 FM) also finds mention here.

I also love 'Blossoms', which is light and innocent and casts so much sunshiny happiness on what could have otherwise been a pretty sombre collection.

To end, I do hope Rupa Publications continues with this initiative—to seek and find beautiful love stories—with the same single-minded, optimistic, never-say-die focus with which we should go through life, seeking love itself.

And everybody who entered the contest, thank you so much for giving me that exclusive peep into your hearts and minds.

Much love,
Anuja Chauhan

Phoenix Mills

Aurodeep Nandi

THE PEOPLE visiting Phoenix Mills mall in Mumbai during the evenings can be broadly categorized into two types—the office-weary, sweaty-shirt folks, and the rest of the world. In the former category are those who have spent most of the day sandwiched between a self-important plastic revolving chair and a computer.

Phoenix Mills, as the mall is known in popular parlance, is a stone's throw from the neighbouring office districts of Worli, Lower Parel and Mahalaxmi, where huge glossy buildings have been erected as elegant tombstones to erstwhile Bombay's dead mills. Phoenix Mills, too, has a similar story—all that remains of its factory days is a tall chimney kept intact cruelly to witness the glitzy decadence eat into what was once the livelihood of thousands of workers.

Come evening, and office-goers from South Mumbai swarm the mall; their overweight, ungainly anatomy pulled into high definition by the heavy bags that they carry on their backs like natural extensions to their spines. As much as I hated it, my own sweaty shirt and black backpack firmly placed me in this category.

My association with Phoenix Mills wasn't all that premeditated. It started innocently enough with office team lunches. Being fifteen minutes away from my workplace meant being whisked into the back seat of the boss's BMW, along with two other minion members of the team, all trying to crack jokes and make merry out of the unremarkable situation. Over the next six months, it was like the restaurant section of the mall—Noodle Bar, Spaghetti Kitchen, Bombay Blues, Dominos, Natural Ice Cream, Baskin Robbins—had been a part of my primary education. Soon, picking up the now familiar menu cards turned out to be a mere formality.

This, however, came at the cost of an expanding girth. Sayoni could tell; she would often complain how it was becoming increasingly difficult to circumscribe her arm around me.

Sayoni. She, too, ran in the credits of Phoenix Mills. She had later admitted that the first time she had spotted me at a distance while waiting for our Facebook-ordained rendezvous at Phoenix Mills, she had had a very strong urge to run. Evidently, my atrociously bright shirt, huge black bag and swaying belly had almost scared her away. She was texting her best friend as to how to covertly make a quick exit, who in turn—bless her—advised her to stay put. Sayoni took the chance and despite my misguided sartorial statement, eventually found me adequately tolerable.

My idea of a girlfriend at the time was somebody who would emerge stunningly out of the reels of a movie or from the pages of an erotic magazine. Sayoni, at her best, looked like the girl who would look dejectedly at the mirror during the first thirty seconds of a fairness cream commercial, wondering if she could ever make it big in the world with her ordinary looks.

So we weren't the movie stars we had each dreamt of dating. And we had started our relationship by telling each other that this was nothing serious—we were just two bored people having some innocent fun.

It was with Sayoni that I discovered Phoenix Mills beyond the obvious. Phoenix, with its huge shops and open courtyard in the middle, metamorphosed into a giant playground where we could roam about after a day's toil like flapping penguins.

Soon, Phoenix became a part of our lives. We would go to watch films at PVR Cinemas upstairs—debating over whether to go for an action flick or some boring abstract film that gave Sayoni a sense of intellectual superiority over me. Ultimately we would, inadvertently, end up opting for unsung movies where the hall would have a greater chance of being empty. In dark, empty theatres, Sayoni would rest her head on my shoulders. The first time she did that, it addled my brains so much that my shoulders froze in military attention, almost bouncing her head back! But the shoulders eventually relaxed. My arm first ventured haltingly and then went more confidently around her. As movies came and went, that roving arm discovered forbidden territories as it remained slung behind her. There was that one instance where we both were crazed enough for her to disappear during the interval and return to our seats in the darkness of the theatre, with her underwear tucked away in her handbag.

Movies would be followed by endless cups of coffee in the small cafés scattered over the mall. We would be part listening to our respective day's tirades and part switching off to listen to the nameless person who would be playing tune after tune on Phoenix's trademark café pianos. We would casually watch the world float by us, like invisible people dissolved in the dusk. When evening would become night, we would trudge back home, noticing attractive people walk into the mall in their flashy clothes, headed for Phoenix's nightclubs.

'Did you see her?' Sayoni once urgently whispered on our way out of the mall, pointing an errant finger at a woman passing us.

'What? She...she looks like she is just from school!' I smiled, blissfully aware of the petite body that strutted past us on pencil high heels and a tight shiny black dress stretched to the seams.

'Do you think our parents would have allowed that when we were that age? I mean... Gosh...today's kids!' Sayoni grumbled in an incredulous tone.

I kept smiling, quite aware that Sayoni would have, in fact, given anything to trade places with that 'today's kid' and to wear that tight dress that would have been less forgiving of her sides than her unflattering beige Fabindia kurta.

There was bliss in what Sayoni and I were doing—looking at the future to the extent of the next day, sinking into our hedonism that didn't require us to look beyond that. But not looking at the future didn't necessarily imply staving it off. Staying with Sayoni, I realized that there came a time in every suitably long relationship when there were only two roads available—either to commit to that person and make a touching story out of our lives, or to part ways and go from intimate people to complete and intimidating strangers. I wasn't quite aware of the exact trigger, but it seemed that Sayoni and I were subconsciously drifting into the latter path. Questions that didn't matter earlier started cropping up with increasing frequency. Pedantic questions like: What do you call this exactly? Were we going to eternally keep sneaking into cinema halls and discreetly find ways of feeling each other up? What was going to happen next? Or was there no next for us? The questions only got bigger and scarier, ultimately engulfing both of us in their confused wake.

The pronoun 'us' soon became two individual and disparate 'I's, while Phoenix Mills looked on helplessly.

After Sayoni's departure from my life, I felt a huge vacuum. All of a sudden, the evening that had a schedule and program to it—thanks to Sayoni's meticulous ways—now seemed completely untethered. Every day as six approached, I would keep wondering what to do next with the rest of the evening. As if under a trance, I would catch a taxi to Phoenix Mills. Post our break-up, I took to the mall like it was an intoxicating, mind-numbing alcoholic drink.

I would go walking about the mall, past the hotspots that Sayoni and I had traversed together in happy abandon. I would sit in the café with the empty seat on the opposite side, listening to the anonymous pianist working the keys. I would watch other couples romance, argue, joke, laugh and cry, as if unaware of the life cycle that awaited them. One time when I got very angry and bitter at the way it had all turned out and Sayoni was declared guilty in my private court of justice, I had walked resolutely into the McDonalds at the side of the mall and gobbled, in quick succession, several burgers, chocolate milkshakes, and mouthfuls of French fries. Fifteen minutes of hectic gluttony later, I forgave Sayoni in an 'out of court settlement' and amicably decided it was my fault too, and that it was all for the better.

After a while, I started avoiding Phoenix Mills altogether. It was as if the mall had too many of my secrets locked up in its walls. It was as if the shop assistants knew of a story that I didn't want them to be privy to. It seemed as if the café pianist were addressing his odes to me. The mall reeked of a familiarity that I had learned to dread. There was something hollow, ghostly and empty in the mall—despite the crowds—that unnerved me. Phoenix soon drifted away from my office-to-home route.

I took my drink and roamed the banquet hall, looking for another person to meet. I was at my university's alumni meet at a suburban hotel and had just rid myself of two people trying to outdo each other in their know-how of financial markets. Free from my obligation to keep nodding and pretending that I cared deeply about the future of the global economy, I spotted Kaveri. Of course, I didn't know her name then. All I saw were two girls talking to each other so stand-offishly that it seemed like they had bored each other to death. The more attractive of them was Kaveri.

Alumni meets are a bit like Dashing Cars—there is a blanket amnesty for simply barging into conversations. Within the first few seconds of introducing myself, I realized that Kaveri could smile so charmingly that it could give Julia Roberts a run for her money. In the next few seconds, I also realized that she was tall. There was something about tall women that always made me weak in the knees. Maybe it was about a subtle symbolism of something remaining tauntingly beyond my reach. Kaveri was dressed very simply—her shirt was a curious and undefined shade of white and her long black skirt reached up to her ankles.

I noticed the sticker on her dress that read '2003-04', which I mentally calculated, made her five years my senior. 'You've got to be kidding me,' a voice in me spoke. 'She looks so young.'

We both hit it off like we had known each other for ages. Half an hour later, in the mercurial and transitory world of alumni meetings, we were still talking. 'I am married,' she had mentioned somewhere in between, casually placing the mention of the husband in an otherwise innocuous, irrelevant sentence.

I shrugged, quietly convincing myself that this was an inconsequential detail.

The evening was coming to a close and the hum of the chattering crowd was slowly reducing. I could feel a wave of desperation rise in me, as if unwilling to let her escape from the bubble of the ephemeral moment that had entrapped both of us in its confines. I made a last-ditch attempt to cling on to my mad fantasy. 'Do you want to go to Marine Drive for a walk before heading home?' I tried to maintain a casual tone, as if there was nothing remotely romantic implied in inviting a near stranger to walk side by side on the sea-facing boulevard. She wore a faraway look and returned the shrug. 'Nah re...not today...I told my husband that I will be back in two hours and it's already been three. Ciao, it was great meeting you.' And with that, she elegantly meandered her way through the nattily dressed crowd and vanished within seconds.

'You too, Kaveri. You too...' I replied under my breath and drained my glass of wine.

*

An sms beeped a couple of days later: Hey...this is Kaveri...how are you doing?

My sluggish day at work suddenly became a shade brighter. *She remembered.* So it wasn't just a vacuous exchange of numbers done out of politeness.

Just after lunch…how do you expect me to be? I replied back.

Thirty seconds later, my phone buzzed again. So what happens after lunch?

I grinned and texted: We do time pass after lunch!

Issh…how lucky you are…can I have your job?

Terrible pay, madam. Timepass isn't really worth the pay cut!

The banter continued for the next fifteen minutes. We kept going back and forth, as if playing a virtual badminton match in a vintage Bollywood movie, where the hero and the heroine would keep tapping delicately at the shuttlecock, in tandem with a happy-go-lucky song.

My colleague in the next cubicle noticed my non-stop texting activity and broad grins.

'Kya baat hai, Arun. Girlfriend or what?' he said.

I winked at him and swivelled my chair away from his prying eyes.

I had made up my mind—I wanted to meet Kaveri, though I knew it wasn't a very clever idea. She was a married woman, after all. What if she bluntly asked why I wanted to meet her? Supposing she wasn't interested? How could I pitch it in such a way that it didn't seem that I was interested in her, but she would still agree to meet me?

Do you have any idea what you are saying? rang an exasperated voice in my head. Do you have any idea how stupid you sound?

I decided to try a slightly convoluted strategy.

Where is your office? I messaged.

Nine messages later, it turned out that she had an office

party that evening.

She would meet me before that, she said. Not Café Coffee Day, she hastened to add, because there was one beside her office, and every occasion meant trooping there—she now had nightmares about that place.

'Phoenix Mills would be a better option,' she opined.

I walked into Phoenix Mills that evening, apprehensive of the place where I had once spent so much of my time. I felt as if somewhere there, Sayoni was watching me, clicking her tongue in disapproval. After waiting for ten minutes at the mall's entrance, Kaveri came walking hurriedly towards me. She looked stunning in her tight black skirt, a red silk top and wedges. I remembered that she had a party to attend later.

'Sorry, sorry, I got late', she said. 'My husband had to be dropped somewhere after which the car came to fetch me.'

The mention of the husband seemed suspiciously deliberate, but I shrugged it off. Again.

'So, where do you want to go?' I asked, trying not to stare at her pretty face.

'Well, I don't know anything about this mall...you tell me, Arun.' Kaveri tossed her hair and looked at me.

I smiled wryly at the thought of how much I actually knew about the place. We walked around the mall and finally decided on Costa Coffee on the second floor. When we took the elevator there, Kaveri was thrilled to see the pianist belting out tunes.

We both sat opposite each other, happy to see the nameless pianist continue to play the keys. 'This is good. So, what's up?' she smiled resplendently. Julia Roberts, I remembered.

I looked around and spotted the seat close to the wall where Sayoni and I would usually sit.

'You know what,' Kaveri continued, 'at the alumni dinner when I learnt that so many of my classmates had gone abroad for studies, I actually started feeling quite left out.'

Kaveri had quite the knack for coming up with random thoughts. I wondered what she would bring up next in our conversation. That was, partly, one of the challenging pleasures of talking to her.

'It's no big deal, really,' I replied. 'Why didn't you go abroad for your studies?'

Kaveri flashed a tragic smile. 'Well, it never quite worked out. First the job, then marriage and then the baby...just didn't work out.'

My heart skipped a beat. Was there a child, too? A sudden dent materialized in my fantasy bubble. I made a half-hearted attempt to joke about it, 'What didn't work out: the kid or the higher studies?'

'The baby,' she replied quietly. 'And the studies, of course!'

'Sorry, I didn't realize,' I said, tentatively placing my hand on hers. I wondered if I had touched a raw nerve somewhere.

We chatted about our lives. She slowly stirred her cappuccino and told me how her marriage had been an arranged one. 'You know, I had always wanted someone who is good at maths and science.' Lost in her coffee, she ruminated, 'Actually, I wanted somebody who was more knowledgeable than me...you know, who could teach me something interesting every day.' A wan smile spread across her face. 'And that wish did get granted.'

'So is your husband the human version of Wikipedia?' I asked.

'Well, he is certainly very knowledgeable. When I met him,

he just seemed like a nice guy…you know…just nice. Nothing very remarkable, a decent guy. I think for the first two years we fought more than anything else. It's like we weren't entirely sure if we were married or not! Now it's kind of stabilized. Today, when I talk to my ex-boyfriend and he asks me if I miss him, I am like, "of course not!"'

We fell silent for a few minutes, observing the people around us.

'What about you?' she asked finally. 'Do you have a girlfriend?'

I gave a summary of what had transpired with Sayoni. While I was talking, Kaveri excused herself to take some lip balm out of her handbag and smudge it on her lips. Two dimples erupted on her face and exploded softly. Whatever it was she was attempting, she was doing it in slow motion, mounting it into a supremely erotic scene. I tried to look elsewhere.

It was getting late for her party. We walked back from the café on the first floor to the taxi stand outside. I couldn't help wonder how people viewed us. To the outside world we probably looked like one of the many couples who were wandering about in the mall. Yet, the two of us had different stories, different lives—faintly connected by an alma mater and a friendly chat over coffee. We went back in the same cab without striking further conversation. When I dropped her off at the party venue, I fumbled for words, bidding her adieu with a tepid handshake.

On my way home, I received a message: Hey, nice to have met you again…

My heart gave a, now familiar, skipped beat.

Likewise. I texted back.

As the cab rattled over the potholed roads to my house in

suburban Mumbai, I couldn't help wishing our meeting had ended on a different note. I now wished that her text message had been replaced by a kiss. I wished everything else could have transformed into a blur: the interrupting party, the Encyclopedic husband, unruly thoughts of Sayoni...

I wished Kaveri and I could nervously, and then hungrily, touch each other, discovering what lay hidden underneath the layers of words that we kept spewing out to one another.

I knew I was being a fool. Yet, somewhere inside me, I fervently wished her to be as big a fool as I.

In the weeks that followed, our volley of messages continued unabashed, becoming the seasoning for many a drab day. And we continued to meet in Phoenix Mills.

It had all started when she had once messaged: Do you like Bob Dylan?

I replied: Ya...I guess...I mean I've just heard a few of his songs.

I love his songs! she squealed her reply.

Girls always have a thing about guys with guitars. I winked my response.

But I really don't like him as a person. I think he is a jerk.

Her response surprised me. Why? I texted back.

Because of what he did with Joan Baez. Very un-rock star like.

My brows furrowed. Who is Joan Baez? I typed.

A beautiful and gifted American musician who was in love with Dylan.

And...?? I didn't know where this was going.

Her biggest mistake was to fall in love with Dylan...it ruined her career and worse ...she became known as Dylan's mistress...

But was it Dylan's fault entirely? I asked, wondering why this upset her so much.

Kaveri's response came after five minutes: *Of course. He led her on and then dumped her.*

I squirmed in my seat. *You know, most guys also feel bad when it doesn't work out.*

I added a rejoinder when Kaveri didn't respond: *Who knows what situation Dylan must have been in at that time? Maybe he was stuck in a bad marriage or something?*

This time Kaveri was quick to reply: *Either have the balls to come out of something you don't want or be fully in it. All this middle-of-the-road, I am helpless thing…I have no sympathy for.*

But Kaveri is life, indeed, so black and white? Some things can't be explained. I messaged back. So many weeks of keypad practice had increased my texting speed.

Hmm…don't know, buzzed Kaveri's reply. *I can't let Dylan off the hook.*

I stared at the message as if the English letters were hieroglyphs that were trying to communicate something beyond the obvious to me.

I took a loo break and came back to my desk. I picked up my phone and finally replied, *You know that you are very boring, don't you?*

I only got a smiley in response. Ah, the conversational full stop!

I immediately fired: *You always send a smiley whenever you want the other person to shut up.*

Kaveri's response came after ten agonizing minutes: *You've started knowing me too well. Just too well.*

After that day, the frequency of Kaveri's messages significantly went down. There was a kind of reserved tone to them and she wouldn't reply back for long periods. My 'are-you-free-to-meet-up' messages were almost certainly doomed to a kamikaze destiny. I felt desperate. Could I complain? What should I complain about? That it was all due to a stupid debate around Bob Dylan? Who was I in her scheme of things, after all? Just a random guy with whom she had had a few cups of coffee and who could make her laugh every now and then? How could I *demand* anything? Maybe she really *was* busy. 'Of course, she's busy,' a voice in my head snarled. 'She is busy being married, you fool!'

Kaveri had gone to her home town in West Bengal for a vacation. I got to know of this in one of the episodic message exchanges that we had had a few days before she left. There were no messages after this—it was as if I didn't exist at all for her. The badminton matches were over. Lunchtime, once again, became only about food. Julia Roberts had become but a distant memory. An all-too-familiar vacuum invaded my life, yet again.

After a few days of desultory silence, I decided to go to my old haunt at Phoenix Mills. I sat there sipping the cardamom-laced hot chocolate at an exorbitantly expensive café, soaking in the melancholic strains of the pianist belting out tunes to his nameless audience.

'What was I even thinking?' I berated myself, feeling the pungency of the cardamom pervading my mouth. I imagined Kaveri in Kolkata, mollycoddled by overprotective, garrulous mothers, aunts, and cousins. And silently in the background would be seated the typically sagacious Bengali menfolk, wilting under the cacophonic domination of their overzealous spouses. I tried to imagine what would happen to that homely scene if I were to suddenly walk into the room. Would she introduce us as a couple? I could now imagine how shocked each one of these characters would look, what kind of noises they would make, and how they would all act horrified, as if put in a real life paranormal film!

I then imagined how the scene would play out in my house. Could I pluck the courage to tell my parents that their son was dating a married woman, five years his senior? Nah… pandemonium would unleash.

Hours passed and my wristwatch's long needle moved from eight to nine, and from nine to ten. And with each passing hour, I noticed how the lights in the mall switched off one by one. The person moonlighting as a doctor in the cosmetic shop on the side took off his white coat, covered the counters with red plastic sheets, and switched off the lights. From my corner at the coffee shop, I was amazed to see a pallid colour fill Phoenix. I had never seen it stripped off its bright lights before. I arched over the sofa to watch the flow of the pretty people trickle out of the golden empire in twos and threes, all preoccupied in their own worlds, returning to the woodwork of their homes, families and all the banality that they had briefly emerged from.

I felt as if Phoenix was communicating to me. The milling crowds, the shutting shops, the disappearing lights—all seemed to carry a message: the baggage had been carried for far too long. Probably it was time to drop it, surrender, and move on.

I sighed and looked around. One of the waiters was looking expectantly in my direction, as if he had been waiting all that while for that one glance from me. I flashed him a tired smile and mouthed: 'BILL'.

This story won the first prize in the Rupa Romance Contest.

Just One Glance

Rhiti Bose

$\mathcal{I}$ LOOKED in the mirror one more time. Hair tied neatly, big round glasses covering half my face. I looked as beautiful as a girl could look with buck teeth and skinny arms. I sighed to myself and turned around. At least I had a new polka-dotted dress in cream and green. Maybe, today he'll notice me? As I went down the stairs, I could feel my heart humming a soft tune.

'Where are you going, Ayesha?' my mother said.

'Ishh Ma, don't you know you should never call from behind? It's bad luck,' I said, feeling a trifle annoyed.

I could see my mother was suppressing half a smile. 'Well, may I know where on earth you are going that you need luck so badly?'

'Nowhere in particular, ma. Tiadidi and I are just going to the main road to have some panipuri.' I stomped out of the house before she could say anything more.

As luck would have it, my best friend, my confidante and my next-door neighbour, Tiadidi, was late as usual. I kept knocking at her bedroom door till she shouted back: 'WAIT, I'm changing!' Tiadidi was only two years older than me, but seemed way much cooler.

'Why aren't you ready yet?' I demanded. 'We'll be late.'

'Late for what? We don't have an appointment with the panipuriwallah. Do we, silly?' she retorted. Her door flew open and I just stood there admiring Tiadidi, as if I were seeing her for the first time. She was beautiful, my Tiadidi; long silky hair, deep black eyes, and everything else, just about perfect.

I swallowed my answer, I hadn't told her yet. It was not the panipuriwallah, but someone else who pulled me out of my house every evening; the reason I kept looking at my mirror, the reason I listened to Udit Narayan and Alka Yagnik's syrupy love songs. I suppressed a sigh and waited impatiently for my friend.

I looked at my wristwatch. It was 5 p.m. I always stepped out at this hour because I knew it was that time of the day when all the local boys would be pounding football at the playground. And amongst them would be *the* boy, rather, *man* of my dreams—the one and only man whom I had loved in this young life of mine. His eyes deep as night, his hair thick as....

'Chal, let's go,' Tiadidi pulled my arm.

I snapped out of my daydream, colour rising to my cheeks.

Tiadidi shot me a quizzical look. 'What happened?' she said.

I quickly composed myself and said, 'Nothing, Tiadidi. Yes, let's go, I can't wait to eat panipuri.'

The panipuriwallah, who had been around in our Barrackpore neighbourhood for as long back as I could remember, had now put up his stall across the main road, which was a little walk away from our respective houses. On our way would come the playground and 'The Local Boys' Club'. I could hardly wait.

As we turned the corner, the playground came into our line of vision. A bunch of boys were running about with a football, and there he was, my hero, my dream guy—but why was he not playing? And who was that with him? I squinted my eyes and pushed up my glasses that I had started wearing since I turned fifteen three weeks back. My heart sank. He was talking to a pretty girl, just about my age. I felt sick and angry. This is what jealousy felt like, I thought. Like a serpent hissing just underneath my brain. Didn't I tell my mother it was bad luck to call me from behind? Again, my anger got directed at her.

'Why is your face all funny?' Tiadidi asked. How well she could read me!

'Nothing,' I replied, struggling to suppress my tears. 'I think something got into my eyes. Come, let's go to the panipuriwallah.'

But I couldn't fool Tiadidi. She knew me too well to realize that I was lying. I knew she would gruel me later when we were back home. As we walked past the girl and *my* guy, everything turned into a blur, leaving a throbbing pain in my stomach. The panipuri tasted like grass, the road back seemed very long and the world seemed to have ended. On our way back home, my eyes casually scanned the playground. Though many others were still playing, my guy had left—probably with his pretty girlfriend, to have rosogollas or something, I thought angrily.

Three weeks had passed since I had seen him with the pretty girl. Irrational anger, hurt and fear kept me away from the playground during the evenings. My sullen face and depressed demeanour didn't go unnoticed by my parents. I even heard my mom whispering to my dad, 'Hormones, she'll get over it.' Suddenly, the fifteen years of my life seemed too long. I was now in a hurry to grow up and move away from this silly old town.

Amidst all the adolescent pain I was experiencing and adding to my silent lovelorn agony, my mother delivered more bad news. One day, Ma came and told me she had enrolled me for maths tuition as my grades had been falling lately and it was time to prepare more seriously for my Board exams that were coming up next year. I wanted to tell her, 'It's not my brain, Ma, but my heart which has stopped working. No amount of tuition can heal it.'

But how wrong I was! God bless my mom for enrolling me in the maths tuition. For, on the first day, there he was, sitting in the midst of seven other kids, his face scrunched in concentration as our tutor explained Trignometry. I felt my heart leap.

Life was looking up once more.

'Why are you grinning so much?' my mother hissed under her breath as she finished the formalities of paying the fee to my tutor. I quickly zipped my mouth and took a seat in my tutor's living room. Suddenly, a forgotten thought reappeared like a pin and burst my present happy bubble. Who had been that girl with him in the playground? Hmm...

Anyway, for now I was just content that I could look at him for two hours straight, three days a week. Ah, bliss.

I returned home that evening, positively happy. When Tiadidi came by the next day, she also noticed a change in my mood. She sat down and picked up a pencil, and started doodling in my book. She threw questions at me like a true interrogator: 'So, are you going to tell me, or do I have to pump it out of you? Who is this boy you are crazy about?' I was so happy I couldn't hold back any longer. I told her everything. Every little detail. How I first noticed him in our neighbourhood, what I felt about him, how handsome he looked, and so on and so forth. Tiadidi shook her pretty head and remarked with great understanding: 'Yes, I know the feeling. You have to show me who he is tomorrow. Then we will figure out a way to talk to him. This is 1995; we are modern women and we have to take control of our love lives, not drool like puppies in the presence of men.'

Of course, we never did speak to him, but Tiadidi now came along with me on all my ventures, apart from the maths tuitions. She was like my older sister, taking care of my messy lovelorn life. Enterprising that she was, she had managed to unearth vital information about him. His name was Robin, just like the bird; he was new in the neighbourhood, and that pretty girl I had seen him with him was his little sister, Ria. Boy, was I on cloud nine!

There was only one problem, though—he never noticed me. Not even on occasions when I dressed up, not even when I asked intelligent questions to the maths tutor, not even when I told my best jokes—at my loudest best—to the other girls in the tuition class.

Months passed and somehow, a year had gone by. The Boards had started in all earnestness. When my tuitions stopped, I stopped seeing him altogether. I never saw him at the playground, I think he must have stopped playing because of the Boards. I, too, became busy with my studies. After all, love wouldn't get me a future, academics alone would. Those were Tiadidi's lines, not mine!

But despite his physical absence, Robin was always there

with me: in the Sepoy Mutiny, in the rainforests, in the algebraic equations—he was there in all my textbooks. Somehow, his presence in my books helped me study, and I knew once the exams were over, I would see him again.

Ma and I were on our way to the local arts and crafts shop. She said it was important to have a hobby, or at least a project to keep me busy during the summer holidays. I didn't have the cheek to tell her, I already *had* a project, viz., 'gawking at Robin.'

'Why do you keep grinning to yourself these days? Silly girl,' Ma snapped.

My heart started beating loudly. There he was, at the store with his dad or perhaps, an uncle. And then my mother surprised me by walking up to the gentleman.

'Hello, Mr Sen,' she said. 'What brings you here? How's your wife? Is this your son?' My jaw dropped as she accosted him with a volley of insignificant questions. The gentleman noted my mother with a flicker of recognition and proceeded to respond with equally insignificant answers.

But it was as if Robin and I didn't exist for these adults. Neither of them bothered to introduce Robin and me to each other. We just stood there, a mute third party to the animated conversation in progress. Robin stood at the shop counter, his back to me, his body stiff, as if he was uncomfortable. I think I even saw him turning for a flash of a second and looking at me, but maybe I imagined that.

After Robin and his father left, Ma asked me what craft items I wanted for my activities. But by then, I had lost all interest in my hobby projects.

'Nothing,' I said with a bored expression making my mother take charge of the situation. Her daughter will not sit idle during the summer vacations!

I just stood there, watching my mom buy sewing and knitting kits for me. Lord, this is not what I had wanted, but I dared not complain to my mother.

I left the shop visibly depressed. Not only had my meeting with Robin been uneventful—the guy didn't even say hello!—now I would be subjected to sewing and knitting lessons from my mother.

The days that followed were equally painful; I yearned for just one glance from Robin. Whenever our paths crossed, he seemed totally unaware of me.

And then something utterly devastating happened that changed my life forever.

My father, Papa, the first man I had ever loved with all my heart, suddenly passed away. The family doctor pronounced that a lethal disease had claimed my father's life. The cause didn't matter to me—all that mattered was Papa was no more. Thankfully, he had been financially prudent, so it was not like Ma and I were left stranded. But still, she decided to sell our house, and move closer to the city and live in one of the new apartment complexes that had come up in Salt Lake, a township in eastern Kolkata. Nothing was of consequence now; all that mattered was Papa was no more, and when we move, I won't ever see Robin again.

The day we moved, all out neighbours came out to bid us adieu. All of us shed a lot of tears. Tiadidi hugged me tight and promised to come and visit me in the city. I never knew so many people loved us so deeply. In the midst of all the tears, however, a little part in my heart was thankful that Ma and I were moving—the house was nothing like before without Papa.

As our taxi made its way towards the main road, I looked out earnestly for Robin, my eyes searching for him in the playground, in the shops, on the roads... Just one glance, I prayed. But he was nowhere to be seen. I had never known love before Robin entered my life. I now knew that all those days I had looked for him with hunger in my eyes was all due to love. I couldn't hold back any longer and started to cry. Warm, salty drops blurred my last vision of the town which I loved so much. I felt my mother's arms slowly entwining me in an embrace; I didn't push her away. She, too, had also lost her love, she would understand, I thought. I buried my face into my mother's sari pallu and cried till there were no tears left, and all I was left with was dry, painful sorrow.

Another two years passed. Contrary to my mother's belief that I would fail all my exams, I had managed to pass with good scores, and had enrolled in one of the best colleges in the city to study English Literature. Every day when I got ready to go to my college, I could see the pride in my mother's eyes. I resolved to make her even more proud of me. Tiadidi and I had continued to stay in touch. Luckily for me, after her graduation, she took up a Bachelor's degree course in Fashion Designing in Kolkata. I started seeing her more often now. She even had a 'boyfriend' these days! And they perpetually had that look in their eyes, as if no one or nothing mattered, but their love. I would be lying if I said that I didn't feel jealous at all.

The dark days of missing Papa were not gone yet; Ma and I still sorely missed him, but we had learned to live with the loss. I had never realized he had been such a planner, that he had planned all my education with so many policies, which started giving us the dividends. It was like he was still protecting us. That added even more poignancy to our circumstances.

And of course, Robin's memory never really left me. The physical distance between us and the added dimension of, perhaps, never seeing him again, elevated him to a sacred position. In my mind, he was someone who was to be loved, to be dreamt of, but never to *have* in my life. Not even someone whose mere glance would be granted to me.

Over the last two years, I had traded my awkward glasses for a pair of contact lenses; chopped off my oily mane into a slicker, more manageable version. My suburban polka-dotted dresses were replaced by comfy jeans and kurtis. The buck tooth was still there, but I noticed when I smiled, it didn't matter, really. And I was thankful that I was still skinny, as being skinny seemed like the in thing in the college circles. When Tiadidi first saw my improved avatar, she said 'get out of here', and I had asked naively, 'where do you want me to go?' She rolled her eyes.

I loved my college. Finally, I was learning something that I really wanted to know—Tagore, Wordsworth, Shakespeare, Hardy, and Eliot. I had made new friends, and often went out with them.

One day, Jia, a good friend, was having a birthday party. She made me promise that I'd come, knowing my small-town intimidation about fancy birthday parties. I had never been to one of these modern-day birthday parties before. My childhood birthdays had always been about relatives dropping by and eating my mother's special dishes: fried rice and chicken.

Jia had told all her girlfriends to dress up, as it was her eighteenth birthday and her 'daddy' had planned special things.

I was in a state of panic. I had nothing decent to wear, I cried out loud in my room. Roughly jumbling up my clothes in the wardrobe, all I had were jeans, T-shirts, a couple of decent looking kurtis. Nothing more fancy than that.

My mother came to my rescue when she saw my predicament. 'Why don't you wear one of my saris?' she said. 'You would look lovely for sure.'

The idea, as ridiculous as it was, seemed like the only choice I had if I didn't want to turn out like a ragamuffin at my friend's fancy birthday party. What did I have to lose? At worst, my friends would laugh at me or the sari might unravel; nothing worse than that could happen!

So I picked a white and turquoise blue sari from my mother's collection. She stitched the blouse, with deft strokes of the hand, to fit my size. I pulled out a pair of fake diamond studs, a silver necklace, and a bracelet to accessorize with the sari. When I was done dressing up, my mother looked approvingly at me and kissed my cheek.

The reflection in the mirror told me I was no more a little girl from the small town of Barrackpore. Nimmi came at 6 p.m. to pick me up. My other college friends, Siksha and Reshmi, were already in the car with her. I got into the car, greeted by cat calls and whistles from the girls.

'You look stunning,' said Siksha. 'Wish we all had worn saris.'

'Shut up,' I rapped her on the arm, though I was blushing furiously.

The party's venue was big and posh, in some four-star hotel. We girls stuck together as we didn't know anyone. We were hoping to hand in the presents, eat the mouth-watering food, and leave as soon as we could. Jia, dressed in a tight red party dress, wouldn't hear of it, though. She dragged us all to the dance floor. We slowly got into the groove of the party, and started enjoying ourselves.

I was dancing with Siksha when I spotted him. My mouth went dry. He was wearing jeans and a white shirt with rolled up sleeves, looking absolutely divine. He was taller than I remembered, and of course, a lot more attractive, minus the teenage pimples. I stopped mid-step, trying to keep my jaw firmly fixed.

I felt faint. 'It's *him*,' I half-whispered.

'Who?' Siksha asked, looking around the room.

'I need a drink.' I squeaked and almost ran to the bar.

As I was sipping my Coke, a familiar figure drew close to me.

'Hello, Ayesha,' a deep voice spoke.

I turned around to face the love of my life, grinning and eating ice cream.

'You...you know my name?' I sputtered, as if it was the most amazing occurrence on the planet.

Robin laughed, 'Of course! My dad and your dad were bridge partners till your father passed away... So sorry about that...he was a wonderful man.' I was, for once, at a loss for words.

'So what are you doing here? Haven't seen you since you and your mom moved out of town.' *He knew so much about me?*

'It's my friend's birthday...' I croaked.

'Get out of here. Jia's your friend? She is my first cousin.'

It *was* a small world, after all.

Then what followed took my breath away. The boy who had never uttered a word before, now gushed: 'It's lovely to see you after such a long time; you have changed a lot, for the better, of course! You know, I quite had a thing for you back then. Never had the courage to speak up, though... I'd just keep glancing at you whenever we met, but you never seemed to notice. I thought you were sweet, smart and funny.' Robin paused and added shyly, 'And now I can add beautiful to that list.' He smiled at me.

I just stood there in disbelief; Robin had a thing for me? For *me*? Get out of here.

I smiled self-consciously and made some incoherent sound.

Robin looked into my eyes, 'You want to dance? They are playing some groovy music.' I croaked something similar to 'yes', wondering how on earth was I going to dance when my knees felt like jelly.

The evening went by in a daze—undoubtedly, the best evening of my life.

It's been three months since Jia's party. Robin and I are inseparable now, though it took me a few weeks to get over the shock of his feelings for me. In fact, it still feels all too unbelievable and dreamlike.

Now my dreams have changed. It's no longer about chasing Robin like a lovesick teenager. I now dream of the time when we both are old, sipping our evening tea in companionable silence, watching the sun go down and our grandchildren at play... Hope this dream, too, comes true.

Jilted

Cecile Rischmann

$\mathscr{T}$HE BRIDAL Mercedes drove into the newly renovated cathedral on Santhome High Road amidst the busy afternoon traffic. Horns blared impatiently as crowds of family and friends followed close behind, turning that narrow road into chaos. Relatives had gathered outside the gate, risking the furious Chennai summer as they waited eagerly for the bride to descend. The month of May wasn't the best period to hold a wedding, especially where most women in the gathering wore Kanchipuram silk saris. But fortunately the sea wasn't far away, sending occasional spells of relief to the wedding guests.

Samantha stepped on to the uneven pathway in her ivory baby-doll shoes, the maid of honour at her heel, arranging that exquisite white gown embroidered with crystals. A short veil, held in place by a wreath made of white flowers, fell over Samantha's face, the simplicity of its design making it the perfect choice for her special day. On cue, the ensemble began 'O Perfect Love' as Gaurav's bride glided down the aisle.

Gaurav stood at the altar in his dark grey tuxedo, a few

heads taller than the average man present at the wedding gathering. His light brown eyes searched the congregation, as if seeking someone in particular. Stefani, dressed in a short black dress that showed off her long tanned legs, sat in the third row, meeting his gaze squarely. He was the first to break contact, almost immediately turning his face towards his bride with an achingly familiar smile that seemed to convey, 'I will love you and cherish you for the rest of my life.'

'Traitor!' Stefani wanted to scream and halt the ceremony on its tracks. If she could muster courage for this, she would be doing Samantha a favor—and herself great poetic justice.

Stefani's mind travelled back to the time when she had first met Gaurav at her brother's wedding in Chennai. Eric had married Gaurav's sister, Zeena. It was only natural that the families would think of a second reunion. Stefani had been reserved in the beginning, a past betrayal making her wary of men. However, it had been difficult to resist Gaurav. A true Mumbaite, he was young, hip and easy-going. By the end of the evening, he had her laughing and rocking to the DJ's music.

She'd been swept off her feet by Gaurav's attention, loving the way he'd possessively taken over her life. His initial short trip to Chennai got extended for another week. So smitten was he by her that he had even considered giving up his job in Mumbai and settling down in Chennai. An equally besotted Stefani had also been ready to give up her career in the French Honorary Consulate office and follow him to Mumbai, if that was what he wanted.

Despite her present state of mind, Stefanie smiled nostalgically, remembering their first kiss. Soon after the wedding, Gaurav had stayed in her house under the pretext of helping them with the water problem that Chennaiites are quite accustomed to. With Eric away on his honeymoon and Stefanie's old mother physically incapable of pumping the handset pump, Gaurav had gallantly taken it upon himself to help the family. So one day, he changed into a pair of faded denims and a cotton T-shirt, and had started pumping water from the handset pump. The entire night, he'd flexed brawn and muscle until every tub, basin and bucket was filled. Suddenly, when he'd looked up, he found Stefani staring at him with her heart in her eyes. Gaurav paused and stretched his limbs. The air had sizzled with tension. They were hot, tired, and sweaty—when his mouth had found hers, Stefani went up in flames. Never had anything seemed so right till that moment than Gaurav taking her in his arms, and kissing her as if his very breath depended on it. 'I love you,' he'd groaned. 'Marry me.'

It was only a matter of time before they would tie the knot, Stefani had thought. Gaurav was thirty-two and she was twenty-eight, mature enough to make their own decisions. They were both Roman Catholic from middle-class families. Gaurav originally hailed from Mangalore, Stefani was from Goa, united by the Konkan language. Until then, Stefani had never considered that she might have lacked in some way. She was fluent in several languages, earned very well, held a top position in the French Consulate…and she was quite attractive to look at! Maybe her only 'issue' in the marriage market could have been that she was a little 'modern'. But Gaurav knew what he was getting into when he saw her, didn't he? She hadn't been wearing a sari like the other girls at Eric's wedding. Her slim, trim form had been draped in a long black figure-hugging cocktail dress. She remembered how difficult it had been to dance in that outfit. Gaurav had gazed into her big black eyes, his finger trailing down her prominent nose and wide mouth. His husky voice had sung into her ear, 'Paint My Love' while they had danced the evening away at the wedding reception.

The church bells rang, jerking Stefani back to the present. The ceremony was about to begin. The choir chanted like angels. The orchestra was conducted by none other than Stefani's eldest brother, Jake! Her entire family was present to participate in the marriage of Gaurav and Samantha. Her brothers had been miffed with Gaurav, but chose to keep up appearances for the extended family's sake.

It should have been me out there, Stefani cried silently, feeling miserable that she should even care after the way Gaurav broke up with her. *Why are you not boycotting this marriage?* a voice in her head asked. If Eric had done the same to Gaurav's sister, Zeena, would her family have stayed silent? Then why should it be any different for Stefani? Is it because she didn't have a father to fight her case? Tears pushed their way through her tightly closed lids. It isn't fair, she wanted to scream. She was just as eligible as Gaurav's bride who looked pleasant enough, but certainly not a stunner to match Gaurav's good looks. Stefani shook her head. There was no point getting bitter about this.

Stefani felt a hand resting on her arm. 'Why are you torturing yourself, Stef?' Her best friend, Britney, leaned toward her and whispered. 'You didn't have to do this—I told you not to attend the wedding.'

'I still cannot believe he's marrying someone else,' Stefani discreetly dabbed the corner of her eyes with her damp tissue.

'You think he cares as much as you do, Stef?' Britney asked in her usual blunt fashion. 'More fool you for crying over this spineless man.'

'Samantha will never love him the way I do...' Stefani's mouth set in a thin line.

'Pah. Too bad he didn't notice your love—at least not enough to marry you,' Britney retorted and sheepishly looked away.

Stefani tried fighting the sobs overwhelming her. She'd been certain of his love; where did she err in her judgment about the man's character? Marriage was a given between Gaurav and her, the happy culmination to their year-long dating. And then, just when Stefani had thought that Gaurav will propose to her any day, he popped another question instead.

'You didn't tell me about your American boyfriend?' he asked her one night as they were driving back from the beach.

Stefani shrugged. 'What is there to tell? It happened two years ago and I've forgotten about it.' You didn't tell me about your past either...I know you dated quite a few girls in college. Your sister told me so!' Stefani winked at him and affectionately squeezed his hand resting on the gear. They were at the traffic light.

Gaurav hit the pedal hard when the light turned green. 'Mom thinks your earlier relationship holds significance. Nice girls don't date American boys...' he trailed, coolly ignoring what Stefani had just said.

Stefani felt a little numb. 'I cannot change my past Gaurav, but rest assured I never went all the way with my ex.'

They drove in silence for the last leg of their journey to her house. Gaurav parked the car before her building and turned off the ignition. 'I'm sorry, Stef,' he inhaled sharply in the dark.

'My mom wants me to call off our relationship. And I can't marry without her approval.'

Stefani's world had shattered at that precise moment. She couldn't believe what she'd heard. The man who'd professed undying love, the man who was already a part of her family—even pumping water for their daily needs—was putting up a fight just because she'd had a boyfriend in the past? All because his mother objected? Which century was he living in?

So yes, she had had a brief friendship with the son of a Diplomat. But Phil had forgotten all about her when he'd gone back to his country. In fact, they hadn't even kept in touch. But obviously, someone had exaggerated the relationship to Gaurav. Stefani knew that his parents had never been fond of her. At a certain level she couldn't blame them. Stefani's job as a public relations officer was such that many a time she had had to do late night dinners with French delegations and Conuslar Heads. Being conservative folks, they probably thought she wasn't the right girl for their son. Stefani now recalled the time Gaurav had taken her to his home in Mangalore. She had felt his parents' cold vibes even back then. His mother abruptly vanished into the kitchen, and his father sat with the newspapers for hours on end. Stefani had wanted to win their love and had even worn a sari that day for Gaurav's sake. After she returned to Chennai, she learnt that his parents had tried to arrange Gaurav's marriage with a Manglorean girl. It was only then reality struck Stefani that she'd never be good enough for them. Of course, Gaurav had firmly refused the match and had insisted that it was Stefani he loved and wanted to marry. She had been so proud of him at the time. But she should have known better than to rejoice prematurely. She should have known his parents would find a way to separate Gaurav from her.

After the break-up, Gaurav had walked away without any repercussions. None of her family members had dared to question him. Maybe, if her father had been alive, he might have done something for Stefani. Her mother was too kind-hearted and mild-mannered a person to confront Gaurav's family. Her brothers had been too chicken to fight for her dignity. Eric certainly didn't want to get pulled into a potential family feud that involved his brother-in-law.

Stefani had felt abandoned and frantically called Gaurav in Mumbai, wrote him letter after letter, but they all went unanswered. She even tried talking to her sister-in-law, Zeena, but again, to no avail. Stefani had waited for a few months, hoping things would settle down and Gaurav would come to his senses. She waited till the elegantly designed card had arrived by post. The cursive gold lettering read: *Join Gaurav and Samantha as they walk into matrimony...*

Stefani knew what she had to do. Her script was ready. The priest had blessed the rings and was preparing for the ceremony. She smoothed the crumpled sheet on her lap, trying to read through her blurred vision the heart-wrenching words she'd penned in the privacy of her bedroom. She rose determinedly from her seat. A sudden hush descended on the congregation. Some elderly ladies were muttering 'O Lord!' in disbelief. Stefani froze and sat down again. Gaurav had left his bride and was walking steadily toward her with an equally determined expression on his face! He stood next to her in the pews and spoke in a low, urgent tone, unmindful of the onlookers' gaze: 'Stef, the priest will be pronouncing Samantha and me man and wife in the next five seconds...Whatever it is you were about to do, *do it now.*'

Stefani blinked, tightening her fingers around the crumpled sheet clutched in her hand. Her mouth opened, but no words came out. Did Gaurav just tell her to stop his marriage? One glance at his earnest expression said he was dead serious. A pulse beat steadily on that clean-shaven jaw she had once caressed with her lips. He was so near her, she could smell his tangy aftershave and warm breath. His hands were clenched at his side. His breathing became irregular.

Britney bristled beside her. 'Don't you have the guts to do it yourself?' she hissed, as her arm went protectively around Stefani's shoulders. 'Leave her alone.'

'I know you were going to object to this matrimony and halt the proceedings. Do it, Stef,' Gaurav's voice was hoarse with emotion. He didn't even glance in Britney's direction. He didn't seem to care that they had a packed audience in the cathedral. Stefani could already hear hushed whispers travelling across the gathering. 'I've never loved anyone the way I love you, Stef…' Stefani blinked back her tears. Was there a catch in his voice? Did he really mean it?

He continued: 'I thought I could make my parents happy. Obviously, I was wrong. What…what I did only made *me* unhappy. Seeing you here shifted something within me, made me realize my…my mistake. I…I can't do this, Stef…the things is, *I can't live without you.*'

The throbbing ache that had now become a part of her everyday suffering, was suddenly easing. Not even in her wildest dreams had Stefani thought that this dramatic turn would happen. God only knew how many times she had beseeched Gaurav to see reason and get back together with her. How many hours and days had passed waiting for his phone call, saying he regretted his decision and wants to come back to her waiting arms.

The crumpled paper slipped from Stefani's grip and fell on the floor. Her eyes wandered over Gaurav's shoulder to that lonely figure at the altar—a bride waiting in anticipation, with bated breath, just as Stefani had been waiting all those months for Gaurav to make up his mind.

Stefani straightened her shoulders and looked Gaurav in the eye. 'I wish you luck, Gaurav,' she said, gently patting his cheek. 'God knows you will need it.'

'Stefani…' Gaurav groaned in disbelief.

The whispers in the cathedral grew louder as Stefanie, smiling faintly at no one in particular, walked out with her head held high. She walked down the same carpeted path that Samantha had walked on sometime back. Stefani's heart was pounding but she was proud that she had done the right thing. Britney shook her head in deep confusion, unable to fathom her friend's motives. Even Stefani couldn't explain the sudden compassion that had come upon her for the unsuspecting bride.

As for Gaurav, Stefani's lips curled in satisfaction—living with a girl he did not love was revenge in itself.

The Unseen Boundaries of Love

Debosmita Nandy

YESTERDAY, I set myself on fire in the kitchen.

I know it was the most cowardly thing to do. Even though I was severely depressed and hovered on the brink of insanity, I had never thought of dying. I was optimistic that my troubles would end soon. For days I was a prisoner in my room, without any connection with the outside world. Still, I hoped that one day my family would accept my boyfriend and forgive me for the grief I had caused them. But what ultimately made me take the extreme step was the excruciatingly horrifying experience of the previous night.

However, as you can see, I did not die. The person who saved me was not my own family—my parents or my brother or sister—even though everybody was present in the house then. The man my family punished me for is the reason why I am still alive to tell you the story. My boyfriend heard my screams and rushed inside the house through the side door, via the kitchen, that was mostly left open till we were ready to retire for the night. I think he might have been hovering around our house, waiting for a chance to sneak in and see me. In one liquid motion he pulled down the thick curtain of our living room, wrapped it around me and held me tight. 'Hold on to me... hold on to me...I will not let you die...' I still hear his words ringing in my ears. This is all I remember from those seconds when the fire started licking me. I must have lost consciousness around that time.

Tell more, do I hear you say? Well, let go back to the beginning.

I am just another nineteen-year-old with the usual dreams and desires. People say I am quite shy, polite and obedient. Even though my family wanted me to take up a professional course after class twelve, I chose to study English Honours in Kolkata's Presidency College, in the hope of becoming a print journalist some day.

Financially, my family is what everybody classifies as lower middle class. My father had retired as a government clerk and now enjoys a meagre pension. It means I need to earn my own living to pay my examination fees, buy necessary books, usually second hand, pay for my bus fare, and eat the very occasional egg roll and phuchka, the Bangla word for panipuri.

My brother, who is seven years elder to me, does everything except study or work. He is tall and has a decently handsome face, which has led him to believe that he can be a Bengali movie hero! So he goes to the local gym and lifts weights to maintain his muscular frame. He has recently started to go to dance class, but our parents do not know about that. Every day, after a meticulous few hours of grooming, he goes to Tollygunge, where all the film studios are. For the whole day, he chats up the assistant directors and spot boys, in the hope of landing a meaty role. There are days when he says he is going to meet some reputed director but, instead, goes to a certain Miss Champa Rani, who is neither young nor beautiful, and hence comes cheap. I know all this not because he confides in me, but because I have keen eyes and ears.

My brother has a huge friend circle in our colony and the personable Sudeep Basak is one of the young men known to him. He lives with his parents in a three-storied bungalow, in the lane parallel to ours, and I've often seen him drive around in his car. He is my brother's age, is reasonably tall and has a lean physique. He is an engineer working in IBM, drives a Hyundai i10 to his office in Sector 5, Rajarhat, and wears branded clothes. But despite being so well-to-do and accomplished in his own right, he is very sociable with young people and respectful toward the older generation. He is polite, ever-helpful and fun to be with. No event in the local pandal during Durga Puja— be it distribution of clothes to the poor, the blood donation camp, serving Ashtami prasad to all and sundry or organising the dhunuchi dance contest, is complete without his presence.

Even though they belong to the same circle of friends, neither my brother nor his other good-for-nothing friends like Sudeep much. In fact, they are so jealous of him that they always tease him about his slight stutter, receding hairline and bespectacled look. But that hardly changes the fact that he is the most sought-after bachelor among the young women of our colony.

I have known Sudeep since we shifted to this neighbourhood five years ago. We hit it off quite well, almost immediately, despite my shy nature and our significant age difference. We forged our friendship on the basis of our common interests in English literature, old Hindi music and Hollywood classics. He used to lend me his books and cassettes, and invite me to his place to watch movies on his laptop. Soon, our close bonding was something that I came to value in life. We used to happily sing Hindi movie songs, laugh together and mimic the boys and girls of our locality, but we took care to do all this in private. When we were with others, he would be his usual friendly self and I would be my usual shy self, never talking much with anybody. It was as if we did not want anybody else to know about how easy, comforting and valuable our friendship was.

Then Aparna arrived at our locality to visit her maternal grandmother for a few days during last year's Durga Puja.

She was 22-years-old, extremely beautiful and an aspiring model. Imagine the flutter she caused in the hearts of every young man of our locality that year! Each of them wanted to talk to her, hold her hand, take her out for coffee and make violent love to her. But her ice-cool persona intimidated them and nobody dared to approach her. The women in our neighbourhood were equally intimidated by her beauty.

Despite her unattainable aura, Aparna soon succumbed to Sudeep's charms. But who could resist his charms for long? On the sixth day of the Durga Puja, Shasthi, Sudeep sang Rabindra Sangeet and Aparna was floored. You could see it in her eyes— she kept on gazing lovingly at him, smiling and fluttering her eyelashes for added effect. As expected, her other suitors were not too pleased.

For the first time in my life, I suffered pangs of jealousy due to reasons of the heart. I did not understand why, since Sudeep and I were only good friends. But every time I saw Aparna and him together, sharing a laugh or talking, I could feel my heart breaking into a hundred pieces. On Navami night, I consoled myself by saying that Aparna would go away a day later and I would have my friend all to myself, again.

But the next day, I heard a rumour that she was extending her stay till Lakshmi Puja. I was furious. I could bear it no more and went to Sudeep's place to meet him. I found him lying on his bed, with his arms beneath his head and eyes fixed on the ceiling. He seemed to be lost in deep thought. I somehow knew, with a sinking heart, that he was thinking of Aparna.

I can sense what you are thinking now—that this is another of those triangular love stories! But let me assure you, this was not the case. Aparna was never a player in our story, only the trigger.

Seeing him thinking deeply about Aparna, or so I presumed, something shifted something within me. I realized then, with a searing pain in my heart, that I loved him. The feeling was sudden, but I couldn't have been happier. The truth was that I was in love with Sudeep. I asked him, with uncharacteristic rudeness, as to what was going on between him and Aparna.

He was thrown off guard by my question. He sat up and stuttered, 'No…Nothing.'

So why was everybody talking about them being a couple, I asked.

Sudeep got up from his bed, held both my arms and looked into my eyes. He assured me that people were merely gossiping about them. I could see he wanted to say something more, but was holding himself back. 'What is the matter, Sudeep da?' I asked him gently, feeling I should now drop the respectful Bangla word for brother altogether. Just Sudeep sounded so romantic and more appropriate, given the state of my heart.

He bit his lips thoughtfully. Slowly and haltingly, he told me that the previous day Aparna had taken him to her house on the pretext of showing him her collection of books. Then she had tried to kiss him when they were in her room.

I was aghast. So, it was true! I knew girls like Aparna were capable of such seducing tactics.

Seeing my shocked expression, Sudeep hastened to add that he did not let her kiss him. Apparently, he had roughly shoved her aside and fled from her house. There was no way he could have kissed her back, Sudeep said. He opened his mouth to speak but hesitated again. I could see he was battling many conflicting emotions inside him.

Without stopping to think, I hugged him and held him tightly. I did not analyse my action, nor did I wonder what he would think of me. My skin tingled when his arms circled around me. In a hoarse whisper he told me that he could not have imagined any sort of relationship with Aparna because he loved me. He has loved me, he said, ever since he met me five years ago, but did not express himself fearing that I would misunderstand his feelings.

But, at that moment, in his arms, I understood. I realized how it felt to love and be loved in return; I now knew how it felt to throw caution to the air, not caring about family and society, and only thinking of your own feelings and desires. That day, I also discovered the romantic side to my personality. Sure, I was confused and mortified, but also ecstatic because Sudeep, my love, was with me. We had a long conversation and promised each other that we would make this journey together, come what may.

I learnt from the neighbourhood grapevine that Aparna left the day following her failed attempt at seducing Sudeep. She left without even bidding him a goodbye. We kissed and our love story took off.

We had to, however, be careful in hiding our relationship

from the public eye. So we continued to behave as earlier in front of everybody, while devising ways and means to meet in far-flung places of the city.

Luckily, both my college and his office were far from where we stayed. I began to go to college early so that he could pick me up from our locality bus stand, away from the prying eyes of people we knew. Our favourite café was a roadside tea stall in a semi-dark lane in Salt Lake, and our favourite movie hall was Ragini in Beliaghata, both 25 kilometres away from our colony in South Kolkata. On every Saturday afternoon, we would meet up discreetly somewhere near Sudeep's home and drive off to Ragini, which screened C-grade Hindi movies. The hall would be empty except for some rickshawallas and sabziwallas scattered around, giving us the much-needed privacy. Then we would go for a walk, hand in hand, in the lanes of Salt Lake, a residential area which is dimly lit most of the time. On Sundays, we used to watch movies and listen to music together at his place, just like before.

Our love story had the thrill of a forbidden pleasure. For the first time in my life, I started hiding things from my family and learnt to make up excuses to go out of the house. I suddenly began to take care of my appearance and clothing. The gifts Sudeep bought for me were kept in his room, since there was no way I could hide them in our small house.

With Sudeep, I came to recognize the rush of passion. The hitherto unknown butterflies in my stomach began to dance more vigorously now. I still remember the day he kissed me for the first time. It was such a strange sensation—the feeling of someone's lips on mine. I had never known such physical intimacy before. Everything in my world stopped when Sudeep kissed me and gently pushed his tongue inside my mouth. I wanted more of him, but he was adamantly a gentleman. 'Let us take it slowly,' was his usual reply.

I was becoming more daring and less careful day by day. I hated the fact that we had to search for deserted bylanes before we could kiss each other inside the dark car. I refused to understand why I could not hold his hand while walking down the streets of Kolkata. I became more demonstrative, much to Sudeep's discomfort. But he never said 'no' to me.

Life was beautiful till the day Sudeep's cousin caught us kissing inside Sudeep's car that was parked in a service lane in Rajarhat.

All hell broke loose at Sudeep's place. Naturally, news reached my household, too.

My family was shocked beyond belief. They summoned Sudeep to our house and both of us stood quietly, amidst the unbearable silence and accusing glares. My brother asked, 'So, while we were thinking you were only friends, this is what you have been doing behind our backs?' I tried clarifying that this was only a recent development, but was stopped midway.

My mother started to cry silently, wiping her eyes with her sari pallu. I wanted to hug and tell her that I was not as bad as she thought. But all she repeatedly said was, 'How could you do this to us?'

'Imagine, what a laughing stock we would be when people come to know of this', my brother stomped around angrily. My father addressed me, 'Did you, for once, think about us? Did you think what will happen if we are ostracized by our friends, neighbours and family? Nobody will want to marry your sister!'

I was hurt, weary and emotionally drained. I didn't understand what the big fuss was about. I loved Sudeep and he loved me, too. I kept on telling them that I was not 'dirty' as my brother was calling me, 'insane' as my mother was thinking, and definitely not an 'aberration', as my father was labelling me!

'Do you two plan to marry?' my brother sniggered. I could not stop my tears from flowing any more.

To my surprise and quiet pride, Sudeep answered for us, 'We definitely want to spend the rest of our lives together.'

I had never seen my father so angry. He roared at Sudeep and ordered him out of our house, threatening him with police action if he ever tried to contact me. I was dragged by my brother to my room and locked up. My mobile phone was taken away and I was banned from stepping out of my room and the house. 'A few days away from that pervert will cure this idiot of all the sickness of love,' was my father's verdict.

'I am an adult,' I squeaked through my tears. I told them that they could not do this to me.

They laughed, 'Of course we can. Once you promise us that this stupid phase is over, you can go out of the house again.'

For three consecutive days, I made plans to escape. For three consecutive nights, I cried alone in my room, unable to do anything. I knew Sudeep was worrying about me but there was no way to let him know of my condition. The next day, he had stopped my sister on her way to school but she scurried away. When she told me this, I requested her if she could please tell him that I was fine. She went away without an answer, throwing me a disgusted look.

On the fourth night at around 1 a.m., my brother came into my room, reeking of alcohol. 'Today, I told everyone at the local club about Sudeep,' he slurred. 'You should have seen their faces.' I knew he was thrilled because he thought he had, at last, found a chink in the perfect Sudeep.

'Did you tell them about me, too?' I asked.

He scowled at me. 'Of course I did not! They would have laughed at me, too.'

He came and sat on the edge of my bed. 'How the hell did my own brother turn out to be a gay? Tell me, how was it to kiss another man? Ugh! So weird and pathetic!'

I squirmed and inched away from him.

He continued to laugh. 'Imagine the shock that the girls of our locality will get. All their efforts at bagging "the most eligible bachelor" Sudeep Basak were such a waste!' He winked at me. 'In a way, it is good for us. One less competition. Oh, sorry, you are not included in the straight men's club.' My brother chortled some more.

He climbed my bed and sat close to me. I gagged on the smell of alcohol; it was some cheap country liquor. 'Hey, little brother. I have always wondered how gay men do it. They say it's through the rear; is it so? Does it hurt?' His voice dropped a decibel. 'Have you guys done it? Go on, admit it!'

In my humiliation and anger, I punched him on his face. Surprised at my sudden assault, he stared at me. Then his eyes narrowed as he caught my wrist and twisted it. I cried out in pain. 'Show me the gay way of sex,' he hissed. His cruel words pierced my soul and the agony of his subsequent action destroyed me completely from within.

A few weeks later

The nurse looked at the comatose body of the young boy lying in the ICU. 'Doctor, even amidst the ugly burns, you can make out that he was a handsome boy,' she sighed.

'I know, Sister,' sighed the doctor who seemed to be in his sixties. 'Young people these days don't think twice before taking their own lives.'

'I heard that the police arrested the other young man called Sudeep. He was this boy's lover; is that right?'

The doctor sighed again. 'Yes. They arrested him under Section 377 of the Indian Penal Code.' He gesticulated at the young boy lying in a state of coma, 'This poor boy had been sodomised brutally the night before he attempted suicide. Even though Sudeep kept on denying that they never had sex and that he had not met this boy for the last four days prior to the attempted suicide.' He looked at the nurse with raised eyebrows, 'Who else could have done it, except him? All the other boys in the locality are straight and normal... '

The nurse looked at the boy's closed eyes and asked, 'What are his chances of waking up?'

The doctor clicked his tongue and shook his head, 'Almost nil.'

This story won the second prize in the Rupa Romance Contest.

The Library

Tarunima Mago

THE SUN smouldered in the late afternoon sky. The bright ball of yellow looked at us haughtily as we mortals scampered about like mice to escape the wrath of the June sun. I dragged myself on the Delhi roads amidst meagre trees, a dozen cars, incessant honking and random children beggars who sprouted suddenly, asking for alms, especially in front of the myriad fast food joints that we passed along the way. I willed myself to keep walking to my destination, notwithstanding the children following me with persistence. I closed my eyes for a few seconds and visualized my destination and the promise of an air conditioner there. It sure felt like the promise of heaven. The kids trailed off after a chase of about 300 metres.

There was the palpable smell of sweat whenever I crossed anybody on the road, making me feel sick. Beads of moisture trickled down my forehead and I dried them using an overused, damp handkerchief. I was tired and irritated, and it took me a lot of effort to walk away from the shrilly shouts of the lemonade guy on a roadside stall who had a smug grin plastered on his face because of the tenfold increase in his sales during the merciless summer months. I couldn't stop for that refreshing glass of lemonade as I was in a tearing hurry to reach my destination.

It had been ages since I had stepped into the reassuring, elegantly done up lobby of the library. I knew its mere sight would soothe me and assure me of the great gifts I would find inside. I had to get to the library that evening. My visit was overdue as I already had a huge fine to pay on borrowed books. I had been so caught up in the preparations for my final year college exams that I had been unable to come sooner to drop off the books.

I checked the time on my watch. I still had two hours—the library would close at 6 p.m. I would quickly go inside, return the overdue books, hurry towards the fiction section and immerse myself for two hours in the imaginary worlds created by ingenious minds. I wanted to borrow new books that promised me new adventures and took me to new places that were outside the scope of exploration in my rather uneventful life.

I smiled with anticipation as I approached the road leading to the library. At last I reached the library gates and rushed past the baggage security check area and jogged awkwardly past the heavy double glass doors to make my way to the stairs. I quickly climbed the stairs to push my way into the library's lobby.

I suddenly felt a little self-conscious when I saw some people looking up questioningly from their books, as if to ask, 'Have you just run a marathon, lady?'

I knew I didn't make a good sight—sweaty, breathless and my unruly curly hair framing my face, not to mention the four books precariously lodged in my arms.

The middle-aged lady at the counter clucked her tongue in a disapproving manner.

'It is really hot outside, isn't it?' she asked by way of a rude conversation opener, looking me up and down with condensation.

'Please let me know how much I have to pay for the late return,' I replied in a businesslike manner. She took the books, keyed in some numbers on her computer and told me how much to pay.

I paid the fine and left to find new treasures. I could feel the librarian's glare following me till I disappeared into the labyrinthine alleys of the spacious library. It was 4.30 p.m. and I didn't have too much time to explore the shelves.

I hurried past huge desks where book lovers sat, engrossed in their own worlds. I saw students diligently studying reference books; an old woman, with her hair pulled back elegantly, reading Wuthering Heights; a girl my age with a Toni Morrison; a young boy with a Sherlock Holmes; and a young American woman with an Anita Desai. I was delighted by this eclectic mixture; I already had a sense of belonging with this library fraternity.

I felt a slight tingling in my legs as I made my way near the shelves; how I loved the musty smell of books! I had just entered the fiction section and randomly pulled out a few books to read the blurbs, when a man with a trolley came to put the 'returned books' in their respective places. I was a trifle irritated with this interruption. I waited for him to arrange the books while I flipped through the novels I had picked up. When the shelver left, I found myself sufficiently alone between the shelves—the way I liked it! I walked along, my fingers calmly tracing the spine of various books in the 'Modern Classics' section. Finding nothing of interest, I saw a few books kept in a bundle in one corner of the shelf. I surmised the shelver must have left these to be arranged later, after the library closed. I decided to browse through them before moving on to the next section.

I was about to pick up the topmost book, when I noticed a few pages peeping out of the novel just below it. My curiosity was piqued and I gently pulled out the book. It was *Love in the Time of Cholera* by Gabriel García Márquez, a book that I had wanted to read for a long time. I pulled out seven white sheets folded in half, with something scribbled on them in a very scrawny, illegible handwriting. I opened the first page and felt my blood rush as I read what was scribbled:

> You know what I am going to say. I love you. What other men may mean when they use that expression, I cannot tell; what I mean is, that I am under the influence of some tremendous attraction which I have resisted in vain, and which overmasters me. You could draw me to fire, you could draw me to water, you could draw me to the gallows, you could draw me to any death, you could draw me to anything I have most avoided, you could draw me to any exposure and disgrace. This and the confusion of my thoughts, so that I am fit for nothing, is what I mean by your being the ruin of me. But if you would return a favorable answer to my offer of myself in marriage, you could draw me to any good—every good—with equal force.
> —Charles Dickens

Did I tell you I am an incorrigible romantic and a sucker for romantic quotes? I felt as if the page was talking to me, as if this was written for *me*, which is why *I* found it by some serendipitous encounter. I read and reread the quote that stirred something within me. I turned the pages and I realized that it was a compilation of a dozen odd love quotes, selected from some of the world's most celebrated novels written by some of the best writers of all time. These were some of the best lines on love I had ever read in my life, and I was thrilled about stumbling upon these papers.

As I turned the pages, the following lines arrested me:

'You. Yes, you. The way you tilt your neck, the way you widen your eyes, the way you pucker your lips, the way you shine… I hate you. I don't know if there is any other emotion stronger than love than hate because that is what I feel for you—something definitely more than love. Such that my knees give in when I see you laugh, my heart threatens to tear apart when your eyes crinkle around the corners in a smile. You drive me mad. More than mad, insane. Maybe I will just call it ardent rapturous adulation or, maybe, more than that. You. Yes, you.'

I had a gut feeling that these were the original words of the person who had written these quotes, the person who was the owner of this handwriting. I was stunned by the impact these words had on me. The rest of the pages were, again, filled with the writer's own words that had such a lyrical quality to them that I wanted to savour them at leisure. I stuffed the sheets into my bag and continued browsing through the shelves.

Suddenly, an idea struck me. My young heart wondered what kind of a person would have written such heartfelt thoughts on love and compiled such sensitive quotes. I tore a sheet of paper from my college notebook and sat on a stool to jot down my thoughts. I started scribbling a rough character sketch of the person who must have written these lines. My first assumption was that the writer was a young man. And so I continued to jot down my assumptions till I was satisfied with the character sketch I had drawn. Once done, I picked up some books from the shelves, including *Love in the Time of Cholera*, and started making my way to the librarian's desk.

It was 5.50 p.m. and I needed to hurry. The counter was already full and I had six people before me. Luckily, the line moved quickly and my turn was next. There was a man in front of me and he seemed to be having a heated exchange with the librarian. I noticed, rather resentfully, that, unlike in my case, she was speaking to him very politely.

'Sir, we have other library members in the queue. I would request you to please step aside and wait for a few more minutes so that I can clarify your doubt. The library is closing in ten minutes and I'll just be with you.' This seemed to assuage the man and he stepped aside with a nod. It was then I noticed how good-looking he was—maybe twenty-seven, tall, with slightly wavy hair framing his attractive face. But I immediately dismissed him as a 'non-reader'; someone who skims the pages of novels but reads *Rolling Stone* cover-to-cover. I studied him from the corner of my eyes and decided he was either an artist or a photographer. But not a reader and certainly not a writer. But then, what was he doing here?

'Yes, ma'am?' the librarian's voice cut into my thoughts.

I kept the books on her desk and handed her my library card. She looked at me a little curiously and then at the good-looking man who was now texting someone on his phone. *Told you he was not a reader or a writer.*

'Sir, I think we found your books.' she said with some glee, as if she had made a path-breaking scientific discovery. I felt confused. Did I have *his* books? The man walked towards the desk, his warm eyes trying to make eye contact with mine. I looked away sheepishly. He had a surprisingly piercing gaze for that boyish face.

I saw the shelver walking hurriedly toward us.

'I am so sorry, ma'am,' he said with an apologetic smile. 'I think there has been some confusion for which I am responsible. I think I picked up some books belonging to this gentleman and kept them in the shelves. One is *Love in the Time of Cholera*. Looks like you have them with you?'

'No problem, it's quite all right,' I said with a smile, though my insides were churning. *Did this man write those wonderful quotes? Did the sheets belong to him as well? So this good-looking bloke was a reader, after all. And a writer!* I silently reprimanded myself for judging him solely on his looks. I flashed him a small smile, placed the books in his hands, and turned to leave the library.

'Um...excuse me,' the man called out. 'Did you, by any chance, see a few sheets inserted inside *Love in the Time of Cholera*? They were there when I had left them on the shelves...'

At my perplexed expression—some acting classes I had taken in high school were finally paying off—he continued, 'I am in the process of collecting some love quotes which I would like to use in my screenplay. I...I am directing a play based on classic literary characters...'

I thwacked my forehead. 'Oh, yes, the papers! I am sorry... the quotes were so good that I wanted to read them later,' I told him honestly, though it cost me a lot in terms of embarrassment in the presence of the stern librarian. I felt the heat rising up my cheeks. I awkwardly searched inside my bag for the pages.

'Thanks. Um…it's all right,' he said, visibly flattered. 'You can take the book and just give me the pages. In fact, you can take all the books. Here, let me return them right away,' he added kindly and placed them on the librarian's desk before I could react.

'Thanks, but it's okay. You can have them back,' I warbled.

'I have already read them, as you might have noticed…' he smiled. I flushed and dug further into my bag. Where were the damn pages?

I finally found them and thrust them into his hands. 'Here you are, thanks,' I mumbled and turned away to save myself from further embarrassment.

'Ma'am, if this gentleman doesn't want these books, would you like to issue them?' the librarian asked in a chirpy tone. I wasn't sure if the smile on her face was one of pity or ridicule.

I nodded, thinking I might as well borrow the books; they were good titles, after all.

Grabbing my issued books, I hurried toward the exit gate. I had never felt so mortified in my entire life; that guy knew I had read his papers and it seemed as if I was in the habit of sneaking upon other people's personal writings!

I felt a wave of relief wash over me as I came under the open sky. Even the warm evening air couldn't disturb this moment of relief.

I traced my steps back to the Metro station and tried to fill my head with pleasant thoughts of reading the books I had just borrowed. The summer holidays stretched ahead of me and I had set myself a personal goal of sinking my teeth into as many books as possible.

Just as I turned the corner of the road from the library, I

heard a voice call out to me, 'Excuse me, please wait!'

I turned to see the same good-looking guy walking hurriedly toward me. 'I'm sorry,' he gasped, a bit breathless, 'but I think you gave me one of your pages with my sheets. It describes someone...' His eyes twinkled with mischief. I noticed his deep dimples for the first time and couldn't help being charmed.

I stared at the paper he was holding. It contained the description of the person who I thought might have written those romantic lines.

But the man who was standing in front of me was entirely different from the one I had imagined. I took the paper from him with a mumbled thanks and stuffed it inside my bag.

He extended his hand to me. 'I am Aditya. Nice to meet you.'

'And I am Nayana. Nice to meet you, too.'

He cleared his throat. 'If you don't mind, can I ask who you were describing in these pages?'

I waved my hands dismissively. I was not going to fall for this trap! 'Oh, no one in particular; just writing about a friend...'

Aditya looked amused. 'Sure. It looks like you are interested in reading. So listen, I am directing this play which I think you will enjoy. It is happening this Saturday at Siri Fort. Do come.' He handed me an invitation card.

'I will surely try, thanks,' I said, already making up my mind to not attend the play of this good-looking man who was trying to be too nice, despite what I had done.

He turned and started walking in the opposite direction and I continued in the direction of the Metro station with butterflies somersaulting in my stomach. When I turned the invitation card in my hands, a familiar scrawny handwriting stared at me:

I may not be a guy with sad eyes that you wanted to see, but I definitely am the one who could fill those sad eyes with happiness. I may not be the one with a tragic and passionate love story to validate my existence, but I sure am the one who is up for that part—however, I do feel it is not necessary to have tragedy in all love stories. I may not be the one to construe elaborate Dickensian lines but I do know that I should appreciate anything or anyone worthy of being appreciated. May I tell you that I see someone worthy of it right now, before my eyes. Will you give me the chance to appreciate you? Hope to see you at the play.

I flung back my head to see if he was still there. To my delight, he was standing across the road, waving at me. I waved back with his card. At that instant, we both knew that I was going to be there at the play.

Rock My Ass!

Shoma Chakraborty

$\mathcal{T}$HE NOISE level inside the room was deafening. The heaving and slithering crowd near the stage were elbowing and chopping at each other in the mosh pit, teeth and bones in the line of fire. The air was thick with sweet smoke, and once his eyes got used to the dimness, Neil could make out some hazy silhouettes of couples huddled against the rough walls, smoking pot or just blowing smoke into each other's open mouths.

Before entering the venue, he'd seen some boys and a girl dressed down in black rags, doubled over the flower beds of the manicured lawns, puking into their shoes. Their friends and companions, also similarly dressed, were either speaking on their mobile phones or smoking nonchalantly, blowing thick rings of smoke out of their nose, or swigging from a can of beer being passed around.

It was just too much for Neil's senses to adjust to. Within minutes of entering the throbbing room he knew he had made a mistake by coming here. He *was* interested in music and loved Rock 'n' Roll in all its avatars, but this? This was just too much—an attack on his nerves! He suddenly realized that his blue silk shirt and expensive shoes were as out of place here as he himself was. The realization made him balk and immediately sweat broke out on his clean-shaved upper lip, unlined forehead, armpits and at the back of his knees.

A thirty-two-year-old accounting professional like him was a misfit in this heaving throng of inebriated youngsters who were banging their heads to pulsating music. Like now, he had felt a similar urge to turn and run away the moment he had rolled his trolley out of the airport and entered the crowded city of Mumbai. Coming from Chandigarh, he was almost choked by the burden of humanity the city was carrying. His work had gotten over in just a few hours and then, finding himself at a loose end at the hotel, he had walked over to this other smaller hotel across the road and found himself in the midst of a rock show.

Looking at the scene playing out in front of him, he mused, 'What is it about big cities that everything that is looked at in contempt in the smaller towns is celebrated as a fad here?' Rock concerts seemed to be the in thing in Mumbai and other metros. He wondered how he had walked into one unwittingly.

'Hey, dude! Move it,' a girl said, poking at his rib with her finger. She was the same, strangely attractive girl from the puke party outside. He recognized her by the weird hairstyle that had made him flinch. She had dirty long hair tied up in a hundred untidy braids. She looked like a bat out of hell, Neil thought, with black-painted nails and lips, and loose dark clothes. Even her T-shirt looked scruffy, with the famous fork-through-the-eye picture of Marilyn Manson scaring the living daylights out of anyone looking at the girl's midsection.

She was poking him again and she was so near him that

her dark Goth lips were almost touching his face. The vodka and puke in her breath almost made him throw up.

'Hey, move it wannabe…' she slurred, looking menacingly at him with her deeply kohled eyes.

'Sorry,' he said, inching away from her.

He stared at her before sliding away from the door into the hotel's throbbing auditorium where the rock concert was on. The group on the stage was a Hard Metal band and grovelling into the mike, starting a frenzy of head-butting in the mosh pit.

The girl followed him. 'What's your problem, man? You from Delhi?' she said. The aggression was apparent in her voice. He didn't realize staring was impolite in a place like Mumbai. This woman was so strange from any he had seen before, outside of movies or fiction, that he could not take his eyes off her.

'Sorry! Did not realize I was staring at you… No…umm… I…I'm from Chandigarh.'

He tried to assuage her feelings with a grin. She reluctantly acknowledged by rolling her eyes and puckering her mouth to blow an errant bang off her eyes.

She had perfect lips, he noticed with a start. What was he thinking? She was wearing black lipstick for Christ's sake! She peered at him again and he realized that he had not stopped staring even after apologizing.

'Sorry,' he mouthed again, trying to be heard over the loud music. From the frenzied response of the crowd, it was safe to conclude that the Metal band had friends scattered in the audience, cheering their tuneless attempt at making maximum noise.

It was the girl who was staring at him now.

'Trying to give me a taste of my own medicine?' he laughed, shaking his head.

She shrugged. 'I tried.'

When she smiled at him—for the first time since they had met—it was like a knock in his gut. He remembered a few football matches when the ball had hit him squarely in the stomach, robbing him of his breath and making his lungs burn. This was not too different.

In the thirty-two years of his existence, Neil had never been sucker-punched by a woman's mere smile. That too, a Goth chick like her.

What was happening? Why did he feel breathless when this dirty, scruffy, ill-dressed, ill-mannered, foul-smelling and drunk girl smiled at him? Was he so starved for female attention?

Hailing from Chandigarh, a city renowned for its beautiful and comely ladies, far superior in beauty to this crazy girl, he found his physical reaction to her quite inexplicable. He had not even gone to the bar at the back to attribute his feelings to alcohol churning in his system.

She continued staring at him, her face scrunched up.

'Are you good?' she said. Her speech was slightly slurred, almost sexy. His blood stirred and his ears were burning from being so close to her mouth. He swallowed hard. Her overly made-up raven eyes were following the path of his Adam's apple. He felt faint due to the high decibel levels and the overpowering smell of pot assailing his nostrils.

The girl tugged at his shirt sleeve. 'Hey! You okay?'

She was so close to his face that her breath was stirring his earlobes. Neil couldn't help noticing her flawless, luminous complexion beneath the ugly make-up.

The room was full of people smoking pot and the resulting odour brought forth a fresh wave of nausea for Neil. He shook his head vigorously and tried extricating himself from her grip.

The band had finally finished its raucous set list concert and was rolling up its equipment. Another three-piece band had come on stage, testing the mikes.

Neil pressed his temples, trying to stop the throbbing headache.

The girl cocked an eyebrow. 'Dude, your eyes look glazed. Sure you did not do any chemical before coming here? Come, let's give you some fresh air.'

Neil wanted to double up with laughter. This girl thinks I'm high and need fresh air. What a joke! he thought. A part of his brain nudged him: Shut up, moron. The girl wants to mother you—she likes you! Enjoy it while it lasts.

An idea formed in his head. Neil cast a solemn expression at the girl and slowly nodded.

'Shit! That's bad, dude. You should never do chemicals. They are bad, you know. Weed and alcohol are fine. Stick to safe stuff in the future, okay?' She dropped her voice a decibel, 'Plus, if there's ever a raid, they'll lock you up if you test positive. Come, it is better outside near the sea. We can come in later.'

He gratefully followed her out of the dark noisy room where the floor-to-ceiling speakers spewed music that still reverberated inside him. As they approached the door, the next band had started its act.

'Hey man, how you doin'?' A dishevelled boy high-fived the girl and then hugged her lightly. Neil felt sudden anger uncoiling inside him. A few more guys staggered toward her and the same process followed till they reached the door.

Neil was grateful to be outside the seedy hotel's confines and inhaled the salty sea breeze in quick hungry gulps. The girl was walking briskly toward the hotel's garden that tumbled into the beach. The cool air was like a balm on his sweaty skin. He wondered why he wore a silk shirt for the flight to Mumbai. This was not a fabric to be worn in a city known for its soaring humidity levels.

He had a sudden urge to rip-off the clinging shirt and vest and let the cool air dry his exposed torso. His hands itched to obey his thoughts, but his strict upbringing restrained him. He had been raised to be a gentleman by his grandfather who had insisted on following Army traditions at home, even after retirement from the Indian Army.

Despite his staid upbringing and years of following a disciplined lifestyle, here he was, lusting after an unknown girl who was not only unkempt, but also an anathema to all that a woman should be.

Neil and the girl jumped over the crumbling wall of the hotel and landed with a soft thud on the sandy beach. The girl was already on her haunches, ripping off her black Converse sneakers with a skull motif. He saw that she had very small feet, pink and smooth with black polish covering the nails. He did not realize that the sight of bare feet could arouse him so much. She massaged her tired feet, while shooting him quizzical glances.

Neil smiled and sat down next to her, taking off his expensive Italian loafers and rolling his designer denims up to his shins.

She went back to massaging her feet, her slender fingers slowly rubbing her toes. Hesitantly, Neil took one of her feet out of her hands and into his. Slowly, he started kneading the middle with soft pressure till she moaned softly. His deft strokes now moved to her heels. Her feet were soft and pretty, despite the offending nail paint. He was suddenly reminded of the small auspicious feet his mother used to draw all over the house during Diwali, symbolizing the Goddess of Wealth, Lakshmi's presence in their lives.

He continued with his massaging and moved to the other foot, thanking his dedicated years as a football player when their coach had taught them simple acupressure techniques to soothe painful muscles. She seemed to have fallen asleep under his able ministrations. He studied her face by the glow of the halogen lamps on the beach. She was young, probably still in college. It was a pity that she chose to conceal her fresh-faced beauty under the dark Gothic make-up she preferred. Her hair was a mess but it gave her the careless charm of a hippie. Her legs were encased in oversized black harem pants that were gathered at the ankle. Neil had mixed feelings toward her. She was, obviously, far younger than him, making him feel guilty about harbouring the slightest of romantic notions.

He was pulling on the toes of her right feet when she suddenly opened her eyes and caught him staring at her. Clumsily gathering herself together, she sat up and murmured a pre-occupied 'thanks'.

He smiled at her confusion.

'You are not on drugs, are you?' she asked.

'No,' he said.

'You must think I'm some tease or a maniac.'

'No, why would you say that?'

She considered his response with confusion in her eyes.

'Umm…you are not a serial killer, are you? Nah… You look too preppy for that.'

He grinned. 'You answered your own question.'

He made to get up, offering her his hand. She placed her palm on his and he pulled her up in one fluid motion. They made their way toward the seashore.

'So, how did you end up at the gig?' she asked, trudging her bare feet in the sand, a sneaker in each hand.

'I saw a poster outside my hotel entrance and asked the valet about this venue. He said it's just across the road and because I had nothing else to do, I walked into the gig. My hotel is over there.' His index finger pointed at a building, its silhouette starkly outlined in the evening light.

'You don't live here then, do you?' she said. 'You said you are from Chandigarh?'

'My hometown is Chandigarh but I live in Delhi.'

She giggled suddenly. 'No wonder you stare! Delhi men are famous for that. You can't help it, can you?'

'No,' he replied in all honesty. 'I'm sorry. I'm normally very well mannered but...but you are very different...not at all like the women I have known in my life.' He cringed as soon as the words were out of his mouth. He sounded like a desperate-to-please adolescent to his ears! He saw her staring at the ocean which was turning a black gold in the horizon.

'Did you come with someone? Will they be looking for you?' he asked, concern laced in his voice.

'Nope, nobody will miss me. I'm okay,' she answered after a long moment of silence.

'Are you feeling any better now?' He pointed at her dainty feet smeared in wet grey sand.

'Oh yes, thank you. My feet were killing me! These shoes are very tight. They do not have the same pattern in my size...'

He answered with a raised eyebrow. When she smiled, his heart beat faster and the initial discomfort of the afternoon was forgotten.

They sat in quiet companionship for a long time and when he finally looked at his watch, he almost jumped to his feet.

'Wow, it's almost midnight. I think we should be getting home. I need to head back to my hotel as I have an early morning meeting in Bandra.'

The girl placed her hand on his shoulder. 'Let's walk a little, this is so nice.'

He was loath to disagree with her. 'Sure, maybe for a few minutes.'

He dragged his bare feet a little further and his spine tickled. It was trying to tell him something. Suddenly, her palm was clasping his. His ears buzzed at the touch, as if he had hit his head against a rock; it was such an intoxicating feeling.

They walked a little further down and suddenly, the hair at the back of his neck stood on end.

He could sense that they were being followed. He wrapped his arm protectively around the girl's slender shoulders. She leaned on him for support as they continued ambling along the beach, almost empty now. Neil was totally distracted by her softness when a hand punched him on his chin. For a second it disoriented him and the girl shrieked. Then, even before he could get his bearings back, another punch landed on his stomach, making him double over in excruciating pain.

Then the kicking started. He heard her shouting, 'No Mickey, Jack, don't hit him so much. He may die. Just take the money and go away, guys. Leave him alone!' Something like fire entered Neil's side and burnt his whole body. Then, once again, there was excruciating pain. He was hurting and burning; his eyes closed on their own accord and he drifted off into unconsciousness.

The smell of the hospital had always been associated with his childhood nightmares. Daddy in the hospital bed, tubes running through his arms, machines beeping around him. The smell—the overpowering smell of death. *I am dying*, Neil thought as he flitted in and out of consciousness, *just like Daddy*.

Neil tried to feel his body with his hands, and his tummy felt solid like a boulder. He was not dead, after all. Not really. He was lying on a hospital bed, valiantly trying to keep his eyes open. When he eventually opened his eyes, he was rewarded with the vision of his mother slumped on a plastic chair next to him.

He closed his eyes again and went back to sleep.

'He is fine. Thank God the girl got him here in time,' Neil's grandfather told the doctor, a young bespectacled man.

'Yes, otherwise he may have died of blood loss. Imagine, those thugs plunged a knife into him and left him on the sand to die,' said the doctor, shaking his head.

'Doctor, I'd like to thank the girl personally. Did she leave a number?'

'No Colonel saab, she did not. She entered your Chandigarh address and phone number in the register after finding them in your grandson's driving license. She was nervous and said her parents may not like police interference. She was so young that I did not insist.'

'Hmm…I understand that but what was she doing on the beach with my grandson so late at night? And why did someone stab him if they did not want his wallet and watch?'

'No idea, sir. The city is full of maniacs of all kind. The girl was at a rock show nearby and said she had come out for a smoke. Your grandson would be fit as a fiddle in a day or so.

We have just kept him sedated to let his wounds heal quickly. I suggest you and your daughter-in-law both go back to your hotel and rest for the night. If we need you, we'll call—though I don't see that happening tonight.'

Neil opened his eyes to a damp and dimly-lit hospital room. He suddenly recalled everything very clearly. He had been mugged and then stabbed. He felt a throbbing sensation where the knife had entered his side like fire.

The girl had been a decoy. He had fallen hook, line and sinker for an age-old trick and played right into the hands of a bunch of junkies. He felt angry at his own vulnerability and lovelorn foolishness. He was thirsty, his throat felt parched. He tried to go back to sleep but the scratchiness inside his throat would not go. Finally, he tried to sit up and search for a glass of water. Didn't they keep this for patients? The slightest of movements hurt the side of his ribs where the knife had plunged into him. He grimaced in pain and struggled with the blanket and the tube in his arm. His thirst was momentarily forgotten.

So the scruffy girl had actually got him to the hospital. Strange! Stranger still was that she had got his wallet and driving license with her. He recalled snatches of conversations between his grandfather and a man and then dismissed it as a part of a dream.

'Oh, you are awake. Are you okay? Should I call the nurse?'

He stilled at the voice. It was the girl from the gig. A petite figure stood near his bed. It was her.

What was she doing in the hospital with him? His heart beat fast, this time for rather unpleasant reasons.

'Switch on the light.' Damn. He didn't even know the girl's

name. How could he have been so foolish to hang out with her at midnight on a secluded beach? Is this what Mumbai does to you—makes you bold and reckless, bordering on the idiotic?

'Switch on the light,' he repeated. It was a command now. He was fully awake. She flicked the switch and he saw her bathed in the room's tepid yellow light. She looked different—scrubbed clean and wearing a white T-shirt and jeans. Her lips were shorn of the hideous black lipstick. Ever her hair looked clean, despite the braids. Suddenly, he felt a pang of pity for her. She looked even younger and on the verge of tears. Without her stage make-up, she was just another kid—no magical allure and certainly not a femme fatale. Neil blanched. He was probably old enough to be her uncle.

'Pass me some water, please,' he said, steadying his voice.

'Yessir!' She felt happy, even relieved, to be of some service to him.

When she held his back to support him while he drank the water, he felt no amorous feelings towards her.

'I'm sorry, I did not know they'd be so stupid, trying to kill you.' Her husky voice was laced with fear.

She continued, 'My brother is into chemicals; got into them a year earlier. As you know, it's an expensive habit. He needed money that day to score—you know, get him drugs from the addas—and asked me to help him. I did not know how far they'd go. I agreed to help him this one time and he almost killed a man. You.' She convulsed with sobs. 'I am so, so sorry,' she said.

Though he was the victim, Neil felt guilty, almost as guilty as her brother should feel for using her—a mere kid—as a conduit in this ploy. He was no better, he silently grimaced. To think that he wanted to seduce her on the beach!

'Are you in school?' he asked.

'No, junior college.'

'What stream?'

'Science, medical.'

'How did you get here at night?'

'Friends dropped me here. I badly wanted to check on you...the nurse recognized me. She thought I was here for night watch since your family has gone home to rest.'

'Your folks are not worried you are not at home?'

'Mummy is in Rome. She's an air hostess.'

'Dad?'

'He's on a tour in the US,' the girl said.

Things were making sense to Neil now. 'I see. Where's your brother?'

She shrugged. 'I don't know. Haven't seen him after the... attack. Told them I'd call the police when they used the...the knife on you...' She swallowed hard.

'Hmm... How did you manage to get me here? Sorry, I seem to have too many questions for you tonight.'

The girl laughed. 'It's okay. I called the ambulance from the hotel lobby and cooked up a story that I'd found you lying mugged on the beach. I'm sorry, but I could not save all your money. My brother...they...snatched some of it away...'

'That's okay. You saved me and got me here, for which I am grateful. Thank you.'

She looked at him incredulously. 'You are not angry at me?'

'No. It was as much my fault as it was yours. If anything, I'm more to be blamed than you. I'm years older to you...just that I hadn't realized it then.'

He tried smiling at her and her face crumpled.

'I'm so sorry,' she repeated. She was sobbing again. 'I...I

don't know how I got pulled into this bad company. It's a sort of an underground cult...they make you wear Gothic make-up, smoke pot and force you to attend rock shows.

Neil nodded. 'It's okay. Do well in your studies and make something of your life. You must quit this bad company and seek the help of your family members. Let me know if I can speak to your parents if you are scared of your brother's interference.' Neil's eyelids slowly started drooping. 'Looks like they have pumped a truckload of painkillers into me. Now let me go back to sleep and you go back home.' He wagged a finger. 'No more late nights at the asinine rock joints. Understand? And no more drinking and smoking pot. Look at your brother; this is how it starts.'

'Yessir.'

'By the way, what is your name? I am Neil.'

'Tanya.'

The last thing Neil noticed before falling asleep was her smile that was packed with enough power to light up the entire city. It was the smile of a relieved and happy young lady who was raring to take charge of her life.

The Impasse

Aabhishek Patwari

VISHNUPANT JOG blew away some of the dust that had accumulated on the sideboard. The first signs of neglect were beginning to show. He felt perturbed even as he was reading his *Loksatta*, uninterrupted for the first time in many years. He glanced around the pista green room that they had called their home for many years. A seemingly large hall, a compact bedroom and a pigeonhole of a kitchen. In short, it was paradise by Mumbai standards. He looked at the thick, red, lumpy tea he had managed to make. It seemed to look away in shame. It was a poor example of its kind and a poor cousin to the brew he was accustommed to waking up to for the last forty years. He rose from the sofa and walked around the house. The sofa had always been *her* domain. His wife was always found sitting there—sorting vegetables, folding clothes or writing household accounts. A familiar sight to anyone who passed the house in the cramped housing complex they lived in. Passers-by could easily spot her through the sheer fabric of the old maroon sari they used as a front door curtain. Neighbours, relatives and friends alike, used to drop in for a cup of tea or for a bowl of varanbhaat. There always was an extra cup or an extra plate for erring husbands, home-alone students, ravenous children, exhausted housewives and bitching mothers-in-law. The women in the building often left their children over with her; young couples, off for a weekend jaunt, left their valuables in her care. Newly-wed couples borrowed sugar from her, while older couples borrowed her companionship.

Vishnupant sighed and folded his newspaper. Although he had never been much of a people's person, his wife had been the opposite. He was snapped out of his reverie as a gust of warm moist wind blew in through that sari curtain. A faint scent of hers momentarily lingered in the air before passing on. He smiled as he looked at her precious melamine plates collection in the showcase. A closer inspection of them revealed that they, too, were gathering dust.

He grabbed a cloth, opened the showcase and brought out all the plates for a final dusting. He glanced at the wall clock. He still had some time before they came to fetch him.

A weak smile spread on Vishnupant's face. The plates were a monument to her rebellion. They were the trophy of a submissive wife who, after years of suppressing her needs, wants and desires for the sake of her husband, children or a relative, had gone out and bought something for herself. He never once remembered using them, though. They were simply there, a reminder of his dead wife. She had brought these home one evening, a few months after Sanjay, their son, had graduated and left for the US for further studies. Vishnupant vividly recalled how his wife had looked that evening—worn out with the happy exhaustion of a prudent shopper who had struck a good deal. Vishnupant was reading a book when she had returned. At first, he reflexively admonished her for spending his money on such a useless commodity. He was a little taken aback when she had firmly replied that this wasn't *his* money, but from her kitty that she had saved up for years from the household money he used to give her.

He had become noticeably softer with her after that day. Vishnupant had never been an unkind or abusive husband. But, as he now looked back at their years spent together—most of it in this house—he recalled that he had often been brusque, abrupt and formal to his new bride when they were newly-weds. It wasn't that he had meant to be that way, but that was how the society had expected him to behave. He had seen his father, brothers and uncles treat their wives in the same brusque manner. There was no fancy 'marriage counselling' in the 1960s. Any tips and guidance that newly-weds got regarding spousal behaviour was through the disapproving, or approving, surreptitious glances thrown by their elders. For instance, women weren't allowed to giggle, a newly-wed couple wasn't supposed to go loitering about town when there were elders at home.

The unspoken rules of marriage were no different for Vishnupant and his wife. At first, conversation was only perfunctory between the bride and the groom. Married at sixteen and twenty-one respectively, they were late according to disapproving family elders. However, lost time had been made up for. Vishnupant had secured a job in Mumbai and moved there shortly after his marriage. Not that the move increased the intimacy between husband and wife, who now lived alone, untethered from the joint family they had been a part of. What the tyrannical elders would have done in the village, Mumbai accomplished the same through traffic, commute and consumption. When not working, Vishnupant often spent entire nights playing cards with his friends. Not that he neglected his official duties or family life as such. By the age of twenty-six and twenty-eight he was a father to a daughter and a son. He was never rude to his wife or ill-treated her. It was just neglect. Plain neglect. Now, as he wiped the last plate clean, he never really understood why he had been the way he had. He shook his head. No, he hadn't neglected her. He had just taken it for granted that she would be there. Tending to his every need, sorting vegetables, folding clothes.

He didn't really pay much attention to her after the children arrived. He had hardly realized when the kids had grown up and graduated. Even their weddings seemed like a blink and miss. It was only after his retirement that he had begun to notice and realize all that she had been doing for him. The little nuances made him realize how much effort it required to be her. He was amazed that he had never noticed her ability to accomplish so much without any help from him. She had single-handedly raised two decent kids. She was the first to help out a family planning a wedding, she would be the first person to console a widow, her presence was widely acknowledged and respected in the small housing colony that they lived in. She had never flinched from community service and yet, never allowed any of that to interfere with her work at home. She never failed to ensure that he had a hot meal before him every night and a fresh breakfast every morning. His clothes were always sparkling and well ironed. The house was always clean, that is why the dust now was so offending.

Vishnupant set down the plates and began putting them back into the showcase one by one. The bell rang as soon as he was done. He looked at the clock and it was only 1 p.m. They weren't expected until seven. He opened the door to a young lad of about twenty-five. 'I am from the agency, sir. I...I was told that there is a pick up here.' the lad said a bit uncertainly. He moved to reveal two attendants in a white uniform. Vishnupant suddenly remembered, 'Oh yes, please come this way.' He led them to the bedroom where the ugly hospital bed was. As they took the heavy contraption away, the lad signed a receipt and returned Vishnupant's deposit. He quietly shut the door behind him. The disease and its signs left as suddenly as it had come, he thought. He served himself some of the watery khichdi he had made for lunch.

It started one afternoon, a year ago, when she had returned from buying vegetables at the Dadar market. She had sat down on her sofa, muttering something about the pain in her legs and an acute weakness. He had dismissed her pain at first but when on the third day she couldn't rise from her bed, he had panicked. An inconvenient commute to the hospital in an autorickshaw had offered little solace. Neoplasia was what the doctors had said. Despite being an educated man, Vishnupant did not understand what the doctors meant, nor did he try. He realized that the inevitable had come—for them to part ways. He had never realized how much she had meant to him until that time. It was precisely at that moment that it dawned on him, in the outpatient ward of the nearest private hospital she had been rushed to, how much he really loved her. The thought of her not being there frightened him. He had sat down heavily on a plastic chair as his old limbs had given way. It took him half an hour to collect himself.

When they told her, she had listened intently. 'Nothing we

can do?' she had asked in her usual composed manner.

'Nothing,' the bespectacled doctor had replied with an apologetic shaking of his head.

Eventually, Vishnupant shared the news with his US-based children, and both of them urged that their parents relocate to America and seek medical treatment there. The older one, Sanjay, had already pressed for a visa interview.

The pain would often come at nights now. And even in the grips of such excruciating pain, she would shout, 'A trip to the toilet will kill me and Sanjay keeps talking about US! Besides, old sick people shouldn't stay with young children in the same house. I don't want our grandkids to see me in this helpless condition.'

Vishnupant smiled admiringly as he remembered her unshakeable pride, holding her steadily through their darkest moments. This was just similar to one of the many battles that she had fought—be it with the vegetable vendor or braving the education process of the two children. But this one was different because it was just the first one he was witness to.

Things were all right in the beginning, really. It was only when she was unable to walk around was when it began taking a toll on her. She had always been an active woman. Cutting her mobility off was like cutting off oxygen from her. Slowly, the number of visitors started dwindling. Women stopped borrowing sugar from her kitchen and exhausted housewives preferred to keep away. She understood, though she never articulated this to her husband. Visiting sick people for prolonged periods of time becomes very taxing. The young avoid it for the fear of the future; the old avoid it for the fear of the present.

Soon there came a time when she could barely sit up.

Sanjay and Geeta, their daughter, took turns to stay over

for two months each but they, too, had their own lives, jobs and families. They could not stay forever and, more importantly, she wouldn't hear of it. When they tried to come again from the US, for the third time each, she sent them packing and later promised them over the phone that she would come visit them soon. When she got better. The tears streaming down from the sides of her eyes didn't go unnoticed by Vishnupant.

The sharp buzz of the bell roused him. It was dark outside and the children playing cricket had gone back to their houses. It was 7:30 p.m. on the wall clock. He could hear the shouts of his grandchildren from outside. They almost fell on him when he opened the door. Two naughty boys running across the house and enlivening it.

'Is everything ready, Dad? Where's your luggage?' Sanjay asked. He looked every bit like his mother but the voice sounded so foreign. Vishnupant's eyes shone with admiration as he glanced at the towering young man in front of him who was her legacy. He could scarcely believe it was the same Sanjay who used to cower behind his textbooks and would go to sleep by the time Vishnupant got home.

'Yes, I am ready. There's my luggage,' he replied as he pointed towards a small suitcase kept near the door.

'Is that it? Dad, you're moving for good now. It will be some time before we come back here. Are you sure that's it?' Sanjay asked a bit incredulously.

'I am an old man, son. Not much to take with me. I am not even sure I will ever come back here,' Vishnupant replied calmly, though his insides were knotted up. He couldn't bear to look at the sofa again.

As Vishnupant stepped out of the house and bolted and locked the door, for the last time, he felt unbidden tears blur his vision. He recalled that although the decision to move in with Sanjay and his family in Boston had been a tough call to take, it wasn't as difficult as leaving this house and it's precious memories.

It was the last month when the paralysis had set in. Often, he would have to spoon-feed the watery khichdi that he had learnt to make, along with the plethora of medicines and IVs. She had learned to live without the mobility but when her voice started to fade, she could not take it anymore. Neither could he. It was last Wednesday when he finally did it. She had often begged him to do as she bid, when she had had the voice. And now she pleaded silently through her eyes. After that night's dinner, he had injected into her arm some of the Buscopan to stave off the pain. As he looked at her sleeping visage, he realized that she deserved this peace. Nine months of suffering had been enough. She did not deserve to continue to live like a hopeless vegetable. The ramrod back was broken and bent now. He knew what he had to do. He held his hand over her nose and mouth. Her body shivered a couple of times before becoming perfectly still. He sobbed like a child, clasping her hands, with his head on her shoulders, before composing himself to make the first of those tormenting phone calls.

As he sat in the cab with Sanjay and his grandchildren, Vishnupant wistfully looked at his house that was trailing away from his vision. Every fibre of his body seemed to cry out, I wish you were here, Ashalatha.

Mixed Exotica Goes to the Party

Sheila Kumar

$\mathcal{T}$HE LABURNUM trees were dripping their bright yellow blossoms heavily on to the roadside as Anjolie Sabharwal drove the slightly beat-up but sturdy and fat-bottomed Swift, which her boss Alan Pereira had generously loaned her, up the flower-edged driveway of his 18th century bungalow. There were several cars parked along the driveway and given the sounds emanating from inside the house, the party was clearly well under way. Luckily, this was a quiet suburb of Bangalore and, knowing her boss's generous ways, Anjolie was sure Alan's neighbours were all invited to the party! The house looked beautiful in the gloaming, its façade covered with wisteria and ivy, with masses of tiny pink roses climbing atop the gazebo that stood to one side of the portico. The trelliswork of the monkey tops gleamed a dark chocolate. Anjolie took a happy moment to savour the pretty picture it all made.

She then rang the doorbell and was met by her newspaper's Resident Editor, Alan, and his wife, Sita. It was their wedding anniversary and Anjolie handed over the gift she'd brought to Sita, kissing the older woman's cheek. Sita was a reed-thin woman with long thick hair which shone a rippling black. Anjolie had noticed that Sita liked to keep her hair in a loose braid at all times, and the hairstyle went, oh-so-well, with the elegant handloom saris that Sita invariably wore. This was in sharp counterpoint to Alan's casual sartorial sense, bordering on the sloppy. Alan wore sharp suits only when he had to meet his bosses. Today, he was in his usual uniform of baggy jeans and a faded Cotswold shirt. Anjolie bit back a smile. He had at least brushed his thick salt and pepper hair, it was behaving itself today!

Anjolie liked Sita, whose dry wit and brusque manner concealed a caring heart. Sita, the neighbourhood's unofficial Good Samaritan, took under her wing just about anyone she felt needed looking after: the gardener's son, the milkman, the cleaning woman, a motley collection of geese, dogs and cats. Alan, though, hated animals; so the geese, dogs and cats were kept in the outhouse. The rest of her charity cases he put up with simply because Alan adored Sita.

'How many years down, Sita?' Anjolie asked teasingly and Alan answered for his wife, in a tone of mock horror, 'Ask me! I've had to put up with this woman for twenty-seven years, would you believe it?'

Even as Anjolie opened her mouth to reply, a deep voice remarked, 'You mean Sita has had to put up with you for twenty-seven years? You poor thing, Sita.' And Rahul Singh came up from behind Alan, shooting Anjolie a look, one of those looks he specialized in.

Her physical reaction was immediate, as it invariably was where this man was concerned. She didn't know Rahul all that well, they hadn't exchanged more than five sentences in the year she had worked in the newspaper, yet all it took was one intense look from those smouldering hazel eyes for her to go up in flames. I guess this is how most of the women in the *Indian Times* office feel about Rahul, she thought wryly. She let her eyes roam over the tall, rangy figure with skin the colour of honey, a narrow waist that only served to emphasize the breadth of his shoulders, and the lean length of his legs. He exuded power, virility, an earthy charisma; he wore it all lightly, but no one could miss it, all the same.

Rahul Singh wasn't even conventionally handsome, come to think of it. He stood just under six feet, his whipcord slim frame was nut-brown, his nose looked like it had been broken sometime in a definitely misspent youth, and his hair was eternally rumpled. But, protested some part of Anjolie's brain, what he had was oodles of sex appeal. He just had to walk into a room for all eyes to be drawn to him. His brows winged their way to his temple in satanic fashion and below them was a pair of expressive eyes the colour of burnished gold. Those eyes were his most arresting feature. Okay, that and his mobile, sensuous mouth, which had a permanent half-smile playing on very sexy lips.

Anjolie had been with the media planning cell of the *Indian Times* newspaper for over a year now and liked her job immensely. Somewhat to her surprise, it wasn't radically different from her stint with a Fleet Street paper, back in London. Then again, the world *had* become a global village, and they were all part of the process. She had also come to love Bangalore, a city that seemed a good mix of the cosmopolitan and the traditional. The southern city had a good vibe to it: balmy days and cool pleasant evenings all year round, pubs which served a mean chicken tikka along with draught beer, down almost every road, and people whose laid-back attitude totally belied their sheer industry, which had propelled the city to the status of India's Silicon Valley. Bangalore was Anjolie's kind of city and she wasn't about to blot her copybook because of the man with the golden-brown eyes.

Rahul Singh was *Indian Times'* photojournalist-at-large, one of the country's most perceptive lensmen. The eye of his camera seemed to look beyond the obvious, the results both startling and deeply moving. Today, he was clad in yet another variation of his regulation jeans, topped by a rust-coloured shirt in soft cotton, sleeves rolled back to reveal sinewy forearms.

Anjolie herself had gone ethnic tonight, and was wearing a raw silk tunic over a churidar, both in a golden shade of mustard. The colour of the dress served to deepen the already dark blue of her eyes, while simultaneously brightening the halo of auburn curls which framed her pretty face. 'Mixed blood exotic,' she had overheard someone describe her in the office canteen the other day, and wasn't sure if the statement contained derision or appreciation. She herself was not in the least bit inclined to either be apologetic about her Welsh mother-Punjabi father lineage or to wear that lineage with an air of entitlement like other Muggles she had seen doing. She was what she was, and others' opinion be damned.

'Hello, Rahul,' she murmured now, trying not to fix her gaze on his sensually sculpted mouth, the mouth that had captured her imagination from the first time she had set eyes on it. She wondered whether it would stiffen with surprise if she leaned forward and pressed her own mouth to it.

Anjolie knew she was something of a sensation in the office; it had as much to do with her being the only 'foreigner' on the staff, as with the way she looked. She had been hit upon, chatted up, and had learned to fend-off advances gracefully, sometimes inventing a special someone back in London so she could let the interested man down lightly. Once in a while, she'd gone out for a movie or dinner with a particularly persistent admirer, but when no sparks flew for Anjolie, she turned down further invitations in a friendly but inoffensive manner.

Despite her newfound affection for Bangalore, London was where she belonged, in the Surbiton semi-detached apartment she shared with her sister, Sue, and London was where she would return in due course. Possibly, London was also where she would meet her special man. She was approaching thirty and was mentally prepared for marriage. All in good time, she told herself. She was in no hurry. No way was she going to marry the wrong man after all the years of waiting for the right one to come along.

India would soon be just a page out of time, a collation of cherished memories, a learning experience in how a newspaper in another country functioned. This country, with its unbearably hot summers, cool winters, its spicy food and hospitable people, its unending fiesta of colour and sound, was only a borrowed, if enchanting, environment for Anjolie. At times she felt like she belonged, at other times she felt totally out of the picture. And never more so than when she was called 'mixed blood exotic'.

And, of course, it piqued her that Rahul was the only man who didn't react to her in the manner of his fellow male colleagues. Whenever they met, he looked straight at her, his face expressionless, a cool smile playing on his lips, as if throwing her a challenge of some sort. Maybe he's not into 'mixed blood exotica', she thought petulantly, her jaw tightening unconsciously.

Rahul watched that delectable mouth purse itself and idly

wondered how it would taste under his. Anjolie was a knock-out: tall, with a lissome figure, masses of curly honey-coloured tresses usually caught up at her nape, navy eyes fringed with impossibly long lashes. He exhaled inaudibly. The end result was nothing short of stunning. She was sexy as hell, too, and he now understood why the men in their office found reasons to pop up in the media cell at least once a day. Poor suckers, he thought dryly, they didn't know what he knew. That Anjolie Sabharwal, not to put too fine a point upon it, was the 'property' of the Resident Editor in Bangalore, and had asked to work in this branch of *Indian Times* just so she could be with Alan Pereira. Watching Alan familiarly put his arm around Anjolie, he thought it was quite obvious that they had an affair going. Alan was her lover, her *married* lover, thought Rahul on a sharp note of distaste. It was a wonder that the news hadn't spread beyond sundry rumours at the *Indian Times* office.

Sita's husky voice floated toward him, interrupting his thoughts. 'Rahul, be a darling, won't you? Take Anjolie inside, give her a drink, introduce her to whoever she doesn't already know.' Rahul stepped forward unsmiling and offered his arm to Anjolie a bit stiffly. She stared at the arm. I can't touch him, she thought frantically, I can't.

Alan and Sita had moved on to greet other guests. The silence stretched, became fraught, and then Rahul asked in a puzzled voice, 'Anjolie? Shall we go in?' Anjolie stood immobile till he laid a gentle hand on her arm.

The moment he touched her, it was like an electric charge had hit them both. He breathed in sharply, then dropped Anjolie's arm like it was a burning shard. Anjolie looked up, a confused expression settling on her face, her heart pounding hard, colour rising to her cheeks. Their eyes locked for a long moment before Rahul repeated in an unsteady voice, 'Shall we go in?' Wordlessly, they moved into the large living room, through the gleaming French windows that now served as frames for the gorgeous skies streaked with orange, pink and gold at this hour of dusk.

A while later, it seemed to Anjolie the evening would never end. Her jaws were beginning to ache with all the smiling and chatter she was forcing herself to engage in. Usually, she enjoyed parties and quite liked the paper's frequent get togethers where everyone talked shop as hard as they discussed politics, quite a national obsession or so it seemed to Anjolie. Food and drink appeared at these dos with almost clockwork precision, was wolfed down by everybody at an incredibly rapid rate and refills then promptly appeared, as if all by magic. This party was no different, but Anjolie wasn't really enjoying it.

Rahul, meanwhile, had reluctantly retreated to the bar with the paper's political bureau chief, the office bore, a man who could go on and on and then on again, about the state of the country, its politicians, its bureaucrats. Rahul's usual poise had deserted him; Anjolie sensed those amber eyes trained on her, literally burning into her skin. Maybe he can't take his eyes off you, she chided herself. But why on earth are you behaving like some lovesick teenager?

Rahul watched Anjolie broodingly. He had no explanation for what had transpired by the front door. Then he came to a simple conclusion. It was a purely sexual reaction. He had to admit that he had been attracted to Anjolie ever since he first met her when she had just joined *Indian Times*. He had tamped it down when he suspected that she and Alan were having an affair, but touching her now, for the first time, had stoked the latent embers.

'What are you scowling about, Singh,' asked the slightly sloshed political bureau chief.

'Exorcism,' Rahul quipped, with a wry smile. At which his colleague drained the whiskey in his glass, patted Rahul's arm and proceeded to seek out other victims in the room.

Anjolie moved towards the dining table which groaned with a delectable mix of seafood from Mangalore, the nearest coastal town, and local vegetarian fare, equally delicious, prepared by the cook under Sita's eagle eye. A Tamil Brahmin, Sita had created quite a scandal in her orthodox family by marrying Alan who was a Mangalorean Christian. However, Anjolie had met quite a few Indians who had married 'out of caste' as the local term went—Hindus married to Muslims, Sikhs married to Christians, and quite a few Indians with American and English spouses. Anjolie smiled. She may be the only 'mixed blood exotic' in the office but definitely not in the country.

Techno rock blared through the speakers and Sita called out to everyone to get on the dance floor. The beautiful Kashmiri carpets had been rolled back in the parlour to allow for dancing. Couples were already on the floor when a junior marketing colleague, an overenthusiastic newbie, came up to Anjolie. 'Come on Anjolie, let's dance,' he said, tugging at her hand. She moved onto the makeshift floor with him, trying her best to lose herself in the insistent beat pounding through the room.

It was well after two in the morning when Anjolie left the party. She moved on to the patio, searching in her beaded purse for the car keys, just as a figure stepped into the light from the shadows near the railing.

Every cell in her body tightened as she looked at Rahul. There was something different about him, his customary sangfroid replaced by a sudden recklessness.

'Leaving?' he asked. 'I was just about to come ask you for a dance.'

'At 2 a.m.? I'm afraid you left it too late, Rahul,' Anjolie managed with a faint smile, a tiredness suddenly settling on her.

He leaned forward, his handsome face just inches from her own. 'Go on, admit it. Were you afraid we'd have a repeat of what happened earlier?' he asked, a distinct rasp in his voice.

Anjolie stared at him, at a loss for any kind of retort. Rahul's eyes glinted like caramelised gold in the partial darkness of the patio, his body taut as a bowstring. 'You wish,' she finally said, her fingers fishing out the car key.

'Let's put it to the test, shall we?' Rahul pulled her hard against him—so hard that Anjolie felt the breath slamming out of her. She didn't mind, though. Wasn't this what she had dreamt of all evening?

Rahul drove his mouth down hard on hers and as their lips fused, it was as if they were born to kiss. His mouth tasted of cigarettes, of whiskey and of him—a musky, tangy, male taste that filled her mouth and her senses. The way he grabbed her had been decidedly lacking in finesse, but his kiss more than made up for that. It was a deeply sensual kiss, the way a kiss should be. Pressing his mouth on hers, coaxing her lips open, he slid his tongue into her mouth, clamping her even closer to him. As their tongues mated in an erotic dance, Anjolie slid her arms around his neck, her fingers feeling his surprisingly silky hair.

One of his hands moved up to cup her silk-covered taut

breast, his thumb probing a nipple which had sprung to life. Anjolie groaned. He was aroused; she could feel him hard against her. And the passing thought occurred to her that if he took her there, right there on that ill-lit patio, she would give herself to him without a whimper. The kiss went on and on, neither of them breaking contact, ignoring the very real danger of asphyxiation.

And then Alan's voice was heard, asking someone to go check on the liquor supplies. Rahul tore his mouth from Anjolie's with a whispered expletive. Anjolie fled, her composure in shreds, her mouth swollen from their kiss and her heart beating like it was about to burst out of her body.

❦

Rahul stood there, fighting for calm. Damn, but the woman had him lose his cool each and every time. So, what was his strategy to be: steal her from under Alan's big red nose? Was Anjolie Sabharwal worth the effort of muddying, hitherto, clean professional waters?

A voice spoke from the shadows of the verandah. 'Got it bad, haven't you?' said the tall lanky man calmly. It was his good friend, Rohan Ram, who headed the Sports Desk.

Rahul shrugged. 'She isn't free,' he said evenly.

'Oh, she is, believe me,' stated Rohan emphatically.

'But isn't she—' began Rahul in a puzzled tone.

'All that guff about Anjolie and Alan? It's just that…guff.'

'And how would you know?' Rahul retorted, fixing Rohan with a suddenly intent gaze.

'You aren't thinking with your head, man,' Rohan replied. 'Alan and Sita have a great marriage. I don't even know how this rumour got started.'

'Thank you for saying that, Rohan. Alan and I *do* have a great marriage going.' Sita's serene voice floated toward them, startling the men. She walked up to them, a smile playing on her lips. 'Beats me too, how this stupid as hell rumour started.'

Rahul looked away sheepishly. 'I...I'm sorry, Sita. It's what I had heard all along...'

Sita laughed and patted him lightly on the arm. 'No worries, Rahul. Let me clear the air. Anjolie's sister, Susan, is going to marry Adam, here in Bangalore this coming June.'

Rahul knew Adam was Alan and Sita's only son; he had studied and now worked in London. Sita continued, 'Which is why Anjolie asked our newspaper's headquarters for a stint with our bureau here. She thought it would be fun to get to know us, to see something of the city...you know, witness India first-hand before her sister joins the family.'

'I see' was all Rahul could manage. He felt like something very heavy had been lifted off his shoulders.

He gave Sita a brief hug and said, 'Thanks, Sita. I've got to go now.'

He strode into the night with a new purpose, fingers closing firmly around his car keys. Then he realized that he didn't have the faintest idea where Anjolie lived. But Rahul Singh was a patient man. He could wait until tomorrow—and all the tomorrows to follow—for a woman like Anjolie.

And then, as his car turned out of the Pereira residence's gates, he found he didn't have to wait until tomorrow, after all. Because there was Anjolie, standing beside her stalled car, hands on her hips, trying to figure out what to do next. Rahul brought his car to a smooth halt just behind her russet-coloured Swift, alighted from his car and strode purposefully towards Anjolie. He stopped mere inches from the startled woman, reached out and hauled her firmly into his arms. Before she could react, he brought his mouth down on hers, for the second time that night. She slid her arms around his neck, returning his kiss with equal fervour. Some things were just meant to be.

RJ Sayema of Purani Jeans from Radio Mirchi 98.3 FM picked this story as her favourite from the anthology.

Something About Karen

Abhishek Mukherjee

$\mathcal{T}$HE SUN was about to set. The blazing orange hue of the evening had announced its arrival through the big wooden windows in the room. The thin beam of light kissed Ryan's outstretched palm as he tried to hold on to it. The hourglass kept on the table seemed to mock him as he meditated on the grains of sand passing though the thin membrane: *You don't know what to do with time, do you?* Ryan closed his eyes. There she was, again! He couldn't help but break into a broad smile. He then remembered how things had been before he came to occupy this dreary room with white walls.

Ryan had been at a stage where the mundane routine of his daily life had started to define him. Each passing day, he felt like water: taking the shape of the empty vessel of his own passive, unexciting life, bottled up to the neck, but with no fizz left. Water. Essential, but flavourless.

Ryan hardly had any friends. His colleagues at his bank

barely noticed him. He was too boring to even be made the object of someone's ridicule. He wore colours that blended into the walls of the building. He had no stories to tell. Life just did not seem to happen to him in Technicolour, the way it did for most others. Slowly, the words had dried up; the thoughts, bubble-like, bursting before they could take shape. But his broken relationship with words had led to a romance with something more intriguing—his dalliance with observation! Slowly, by the passing of each excruciating minute, he had metamorphosed into a silent witness of the chaos of the rest of the world.

He cherished his newly found gift. Like a little child, he protected it. Observing everyone, their faces, their nuances, their idiosyncrasies, their twitches, their itches, their laughter, their tears—their frowns, even. He could see their soul, their spirit, their inner ugliness, their external beauty. The simple and the pompous; the grotesque and the beautiful. He took to observing all: the rich and the poor; the humble and the haughty. Everyone! Everything! Every minute!

One such observant minute on the railway station had led his searching eyes to Karen. There she was, in the middle of a hundred people, and the minute he saw her, he couldn't tear his eyes away from her. Everything faded into the background. He observed her keenly. There was something about Karen. Her long black hair tied back neatly, the creases on her forehead giving away her age—she must have been in her late thirties or early forties—the distinctive collarbone, the rounded shoulders, the perfect waistline, her pretty shoes. Everything about her mesmerized Ryan.

Providentially, he kept running into Karen everywhere: at the supermarket, in the neighbourhood park, at the train station. Was she also aware of his presence? Each day he saw her, he took a step closer toward her. He observed her dark ebony eyes, her perfectly aligned cheekbones, her smile. Oh, her smile. She smiled with her heart; seasons changed as she smiled. The air smelled like the sweet evening breeze of spring whenever she walked past. He was delighted to see Karen every day at the station. His eyes would follow her with unwavering gaze—from ten past nine to nine-thirty, when the local train arrived. But he had laid down some rules of the game. He tried not to ogle at her overtly, lest any unpleasant episode occur. You never knew with women these days!

Karen had brightened Ryan's life in myriad ways. He smiled more. There was a prance in his step that people noticed. He wanted to be around Karen all the time. But he didn't know what he would tell her if she spoke to him. He had never rehearsed it in his head. He loved gazing at her like he used to gaze at the stars on a cloudless night as a kid. He wondered what it would be like to rest his head back on her outstretched arms, as they lay on the open fields in the city's outskirts— stargazing, letting the gentle summer breeze caress their hair. He remembered coming to the fields with his mother when he was a kid; they would picnic here, lay back on the grass and gaze at the stars studded in the raven skies.

He felt a pang when he thought of his old mother. He had not seen her in ages. Where was the time to get leave from work and visit her in the small coastal town, five hours by road from the city? She liked living by herself, she often said. Ryan frowned in thought. Would his mother like Karen? Would Karen like his mother? Would his mother scold Karen for wearing high heels? Ryan chuckled softly. All important matters!

As the days passed, he memorized every crease on Karen's face, every strand of her silky hair that kissed her ears. He would stand near her in the Metro station and observe her like a devoted fan. He had committed to memory the fragrance of her shampoo and the fruity perfume she generously sprayed on herself every Friday. He knew she reserved the pink shirt for Thursdays and the white for Wednesdays.

He loved how she was always poised, even in the almost stampede-like situation when people were elbowing each other, desperate to board the local. Whenever Ryan would spot Karen at the station, there would be a moment of silence in the orchestra of cacophony. She would move effortlessly in the swarming crowd with the grace of a queen, not a strand out of place, her shirt never losing its creases. Karen. She was everything most were not—elegant, graceful and composed. She was everything he had always wanted. He worshipped her. He prized her. He looked out for her. He watched her from a distance like a guarding hawk. He would fight the world for her. He would fight the world beyond for her.

Though she never seemed to notice him, it didn't bother him much. He fell in love simply by observing her. He was her guarding angel. She was divine, while he was, but, a mere mortal.

His love strong. His love servile. His love non-validated.

Ryan was obsessed with Karen. Her face was plastered on his imagination. She was the last vision when he closed his eyes. She was the first vision when he opened his eyes. The time had come; he *had* to talk to her. He *had* to know what she sounded like.

For weeks he stood in front of the mirror, trying to figure what he would tell her when he finally spoke to her. But first, he wanted to spruce up his wardrobe. He had to buy new clothes that flattered his appearance. She wouldn't like his colourless, staid shirts. She would like bright colours. She wouldn't like his school-like black shoes. He needed a cool haircut; she would hate his hair parting. He needed to shave. He needed to get into shape. He had to upgrade his wardrobe and appearance before he could talk to her. He had to show his respect for her, after all. In his opinion, nothing was more disrespectful than a man not making an attempt to look good for the woman he loved.

And what an attempt he made! He got up early every morning to go jogging to lose the muffin top. He went to the club to play squash—he had to get fitter for her sake. He wore T-shirts now: bright and striped. In all colours: blue, green, grey, red and all the hidden colours in the rainbow. Ryan made his tailor rich by changing his wardrobe completely. His baggy shirts and comfortable khakis made way for the more fitting, suave, tailor-made clothes. He started wearing a necktie to work on days he wore a shirt. He got a nice haircut that was short and unfussy. And he took the effort to splash cologne on his face after shaving every day. He didn't tolerate any stubble on his face these days. After taking pains to dress up for work, he wore his most important accessory before leaving home: his smile.

Ryan was a changed man now. His exterior shone like a newly minted coin. He greeted people with a bright smile and a friendly nod. He made the men jealous and the women take note of him. Some women were curious and some were inclined toward him. His colleagues changed around him. He was now spoken to, attended to, sided with and made part of their daytime gossip sessions by the water cooler. But Ryan didn't seem to give a damn. He didn't pay attention to what they had to say. They didn't matter then and they didn't matter now. He just smiled and shrugged off all the attention. Paul, who sat in the next cubicle, now proudly declared himself as Ryan's *buddy* after he had agreed to play squash with him. He was ever curious as to what had brought about the change in Ryan. In a moment of inebriation, Ryan had conceded a weak nod when Paul pestered him with, 'Is there a woman in your life?' Ryan and he were at a restaurant that night having dinner with Paul's petite and attractive girlfriend, Betty.

Paul was in his late twenties: loud, boisterous, a tad egotistical. Always had an anecdote to share at the office water cooler. Everyone listened to him intently as he had un-paralleled dexterity in jumping from one topic to another—women, sports, government, marriage, sex, love. He was the guru amongst them. Gregarious and generous with dispensing advice to whoever cared to listen. He was also the king of infidelity. Whenever he claimed this with sickening pride, Ryan's stomach churned. For unlike Paul, Ryan was a one-woman man. Karen was, and will always be, the only one for him.

It was hard for him to imagine why a sincere, sweet woman like Betty chose to be with Paul.

Soon, Ryan started hanging out more with Paul and Betty. And the more time Betty spent with Ryan, the more she liked him. He was never rude and obnoxious like Paul was, more importantly, Ryan always *listened* to her. How could a woman not be attracted to a man who listened to her? It was a bonus that Ryan dressed well and was a proven performer at work. A man like him was sure to attract his fair share of women, so Betty thought! But he never discussed the opposite sex in crass terms like Paul always did. Betty was both relieved and pleased that Paul was comfortable with her hanging out with Ryan. 'He's a trustworthy guy,' Paul often said about Ryan.

'I'm surprised we barely noticed him earlier.' Betty mulled over Paul's words. Ryan had started to hit the checkmark for every parameter; even she noticed that.

Betty instinctively knew it had to be someone special for whom Ryan had changed so much. Out of curiosity, she would ask him quite often how his girlfriend looked. Each time, Ryan would look wistfully into the distance and say, 'Breathtaking.' He was always cagey about her and dismissed further probing questions with a wave of his hand, saying Karen was travelling on work and would return after a month.

Betty tried to shrug off the envy creeping up her collarbone. She wondered what it felt like to be Ryan's chosen one. She was an attractive woman herself, but a string of bad affairs—Paul too was headed that way—had started making her question if men were worth her time and beauty parlour bills. But Ryan was a breath of fresh air. She had never met a man like him—so sensitive, caring and...and...normal. Betty wished to be with him, despite knowing he was taken. She knew he would treat her like royalty. She often tried to look deep into his eyes. It was always searching, obviously for the woman he desired with all his heart.

Each day she saw him, Betty's desire for him grew stronger. She wanted him like she had wanted no other man before. She wanted to sleep in his arms, wake up to him in the morning. She wanted to be loved by him. She wanted his undivided attention.

Finally, she took charge of the situation. 'Make love to me,' she whispered in his ear at the bar one stormy night. She kissed his ear and neck. When he kissed her back, Betty almost swooned with happiness. His heart raced when she placed her hand on his chest.

Ryan took Betty to his flat. He gently lifted her by the waist, her slender legs wrapping around his waist. She kissed him passionately as his fingers traced her neck. Something about the way he held her aroused Betty. He placed one hand on her back and with the other cupped her chin. Never had she felt so wanted and desired. She looked into his eyes and was relieved to find that it wasn't in its usual searching self. His eyes seemed to speak to her tonight, they tried to convey something to her. But she was so caught up in the heat of the moment that she didn't bother to decode the message.

How they made love that night! Ryan made her feel beautiful, desired—the woman she knew herself to be almost a decade back. She kissed him and he kissed her back with a sense of urgency that was hard to miss. He pulled her closer to him, whispered sweet nothings in her ears. Betty was falling deeper in love with him. There was no ego in the way he took her, no trace of jubilation when he pleasured her.

But there *was* a tiny problem. She knew Ryan's heart was with someone else. Though he had cheated on his girlfriend, Betty knew it was done in the heat of the moment. She knew she could not hold a candle to Ryan's woman. But she *had* to know who this woman was. She wondered why Ryan avoided discussing her.

Betty's curiosity about Karen was heightened. She had, so far, only heard her described as 'breathtaking' by Ryan. But she wanted to know more, for somewhere in her heart was ignited a spark, a burning curiosity, to see this woman who had transformed Ryan's life for the better.

Betty had seen Ryan staring at a picture sometimes. It was always kept in his right jacket pocket! Betty knew it was Karen's. Ryan always held it so close she never got a chance to take a look at it. Now that Ryan had gone to take a shower, Betty found it hard to contain her curiosity any further. The jacket he had worn the previous night was draped on a chair. With one eye trained on the bathroom door, Betty carefully reached into the jacket's pocket and pulled out the picture. She did a double take when she looked at it. She felt a numbness settle on her. She wore her reading glasses and looked at it more closely. The picture was exactly the way Ryan had described Karen to be. Breathtaking. Betty breathed hard. It was as if someone had clicked the picture in front of a mirror.

Her heart raced and her mouth felt dry. She heard the bathroom knob turn. Quickly, she put the picture inside her purse. She knew she had to study it further.

Ryan came out, unflustered, relaxed and refreshed. He glowed like always. He bent over and kissed Betty on the forehead.

Betty forced a smile on her face. She looked for her clothes strewn on the bedroom floor. She had to get dressed and be out of here fast. She peeked outside the window and felt her heart sink. Torrential downpour and lightning had engulfed the night sky. No way in hell could she step out now. She would have to spend the rest of the night with Ryan.

She excused herself and went to the kitchen to drink water. Her mind was in a tizzy, still unable to register what she had just seen. She couldn't add up the story Karen's picture was telling her. All she knew was she had to be careful not to let Ryan inside her head. She was falling in *love* with the man, for Pete's sake! She cursed herself. Why did she have to look at the picture? Hot tears rolled down her cheeks.

She knew she had to act fast once dawn broke out in the skies. She tiptoed to the bedroom. Ryan was fast asleep like a baby, the table lamp shining gently on his carelessly handsome face. Despite her newfound discovery, Betty was amused Ryan was smiling even in his sleep. She couldn't help cuddling up next to him.

No matter what, Betty knew she loved the man. This was her last thought as she drifted off to sleep. They both deserved the bliss of that momentous night.

The next morning she left a note saying she had to leave early and slipped out of the flat. Ryan went about his morning rituals as usual, and went to the station to take the local to work. But little did he realize that Betty had followed him to the station.

She quietly observed as Ryan went and sat on the bench, next to the station's coffee stall. He seemed to be staring in one particular direction, his eyes searching for someone. Betty keenly followed his gaze, though she knew Karen will never appear before them. Ryan smiled, rose from his bench, stood in front of a flag pole and started talking to it. Some people darted curious looks at him, two women started giggling.

Betty couldn't control her tears. Ryan was sick, very sick. She knew the moment she saw the picture the previous night. *The picture of Karen was Ryan's own. Only, in a woman's clothes.* He had clicked it himself. He was dressed in a pink shirt, with silky hair framing his face. And what high heels he had worn.

Betty now knew there was no Karen. But to Ryan, Karen was the reason he was still alive. Betty's heart went out to him; she knew she had to report his problem to mental health experts. This was the best she could do for the man she now loved so deeply.

The sun had now set. The dark shadows of night entered the hospital room once again. Ryan took out the photo from his pocket and put it back inside. He combed his hair, polished his shoes and tied the Windsor knot around his neck.

He stepped out into the hospital's garden and smiled at the pretty stranger who had been coming to meet him every day for the last two years. Betty returned his smile, still hoping that one day, Ryan would see his Karen in her. He was worth waiting for all her life.

The Affair

Anita Sarkar

'SIX MONTHS, Namita. Give me six months.' Atul was pleading for his life, their life. They looked up the calendar in her diary and circled 16 November with the green ballpoint pen that she always carried in her handbag.

'That's when I will be free and come back for you,' he said.

Dusk was falling as Namita and Atul tried to make light conversation at their favourite café. Soon it would be time to part ways. Atul was leaving by the morning flight to London. Namita was bracing herself for the interminable wait.

Many days later, when she was herself in a plane on a business trip, she remembered every trivial detail of their last meeting at the café, as if she had been watching a scene in a film. What she had worn (the blue chiffon top that had been a present from him), the way she had deliberately stirred her tea without looking up, the mother with the fidgety child at the next table who kept running up to them, the way he had reached out for her hand across the table. In a film it was somebody else's heartbreak. But this was their story playing out.

To begin with, Namita had never wanted an affair with a married man. You can never win if you are the other woman, she would remark airily to her friends, with the wisdom of a twenty-eight-year-old who had never been in that abyss. But Atul had come along without any warning. They had known each other for sometime as business acquaintances. He liked her intelligent eyes and the smile that played on her lips when she thought no one was looking, as if she was enjoying a private joke. She could always pick Atul out in a crowded room and their eyes would invariably meet. He kept twisting the ring on his finger, as if to make sure people knew he was married. He soon took to seeking her out with a drink. They would chat casually without resorting to the usual party chatter. Afterwards, she would remember every word he had said. And the twisting of the ring. They never made a date but once emerging together from the lift of a building where they had had a conference, they found themselves entering the restaurant on the ground floor, still talking and laughing. That's how it had begun.

The spark was there from their first meeting but it could have been put out without too much pain and suffering—if only she had walked away before the flame engulfed them both in a hopeless love. But besotted as she was with a man seven years older, she didn't want to. All she wanted, all she lived for, were those stolen moments after office hours, when they would go for long drives or recklessly check into hotels as a married couple. Even Atul couldn't have prevented the suffering that seemed inevitable from the outset. He was as smitten, as much in love with her, as she was with him. He was in love enough to want to leave his gorgeous wife. Renuka was a perfect wife in many ways; beautiful, with a talent for being a gracious hostess. But somewhere along the monotony of married life, Renuka and he had fallen out of love, the embers of passion had long fizzled out. They had both worked hard for his success which he owed as much to her—for being the perfect 'foil'—as to his own brilliance. They expected each other to play their part as his career progressed. Renuka shielded him from many of the problems that would have taken away his focus from his career. He was on the way to the top and failure was not on the agenda. But they never chatted or laughed together any more and even their time alone was programmed with things to do. If this was someone else's story, Renuka would find it hard to understand. Atul wished there was a chink in her armour. With Namita, he could just be himself. It didn't matter if they had nothing else, no more goals to achieve. He just knew he wanted to spend the rest of his life with her.

But now Atul was struggling to find a way to tell Renuka that he wanted to leave her because he was in love with another woman. 'I'll tell her after Sid's birthday,' he thought. Or, 'I have to wait till her mother is better.' Or, 'My aunt is visiting from America—after that, perhaps?' Once he told Renuka that they had to get away for a few days by themselves, that it was a matter of life and death. But she just laughed away the suggestion. They were an 'old married couple', she said, and what about the important visitors from America who were expected next week? There were a million things to do! And so it went until Atul increasingly began to feel trapped. The days passed. He hated the words 'carry on'. Wouldn't he carry on if he could? He couldn't bear to be parted from his son. Couldn't bear to think of his little world falling apart. But Atul would pay the price. He steeled himself and made the decision. There was never a right time to tell his wife that what he wanted—and was begging for—was his freedom. He felt caught in a lackkustre marriage. He couldn't be the husband Renuka wanted, not when he wanted to be with someone else more than anything else in the world.

In the months since Atul and Namita had started seeing each other, it became more and more difficult to sustain the affair. In those intimate moments after they made love, they sometimes talked about breaking it off themselves. It was the sensible thing to do, they told each other. They would always have Paris, they said dreamily, quoting *Casablanca*. But that thought would be brushed aside the moment he swept her in his arms. 'I love you, Namita. I can't live without you and I will fight for you.'

Then something happened that presented itself as a godsend opportunity. Atul got a six-month posting to London. Renuka had family there and Atul believed he could now gently break the news to her. It would be less traumatic for her there as she would get moral support from her sister and brother. Atul wanted to do this the honourable way—he would tell her, arrange for Sid's schooling, make sure they were properly settled, and then leave for India to join Namita. He could only hope Renuka would understand. But would she? She was not the kind of woman who would easily give in. She would take the failure of their marriage as a personal failure and do everything in her power to make things work. Her determination, not jealousy, would be a formidable foe.

When Atul met Namita at the café the morning before he flew to London with his family, they had vowed never to keep in touch and even resist calling each other. Namita had plunged into work with a vengeance. As a high-flying marketing consultant for a German multinational, she had to make pitches, write reports, attend meetings, travel. She mercilessly put in sixteen-hour days, took on additional responsibilities in her department and travelled like a maniac, if only to keep from looking at that circled day in the calendar. Every now and then her ever-optimistic mother would send her marriage proposals: 'good boys' from 'good families' based in Atlanta, Singapore and Bangalore. But Namita would trash the envelopes and delete the emails with not a glance. Atul played in her mind like a favourite song on loop.

And though she was not in touch with him, he did manage to sneak his way into her life every once in a while. Once at a business party, his name floated up to her from across the room. Atul was doing extremely well, someone said, and was sure to get the promotion that men in their thirties can only aspire to. Someone had seen him with his wife—'what a bombshell'—in London and apparently, they looked 'deliriously' happy. Namita flinched. She was fairly sure those words were not meant for her ears—she could vouch for the fact that none of their colleagues knew about their affair. But the words hurt, nonetheless. She took a glass of vodka from the waiter's tray and downed it in one shot. She savoured the liquid burning her throat. Atul was happy and every day she was dying a little. But he had promised for his own sake as much as hers. He would come to her as he said he would. He would, he would.

More punishing work was the answer and it didn't go unnoticed. Namita was given one of the firm's most important projects to lead. They said the project would finish on 9 November.

The project was a big success and Namita took a month's leave from 10 November. She opened her diary and saw the circled date staring at her. The final countdown had begun. She knew Atul would come back for her. She could feel it in her bones. Namita wanted everything to be perfect to welcome him. She reupholstered the sofas, stocked up on his favourite wines and bought fresh linen, remembering to include a red towel set because he loved the colour. She then indulged in some spa treatment for herself to beat the nerves. She looked radiant and she knew this was not because of expensive beauty treatments. In less than a week, she would be in his arms—the closest thing to heaven. Nothing else mattered.

The early morning skies were streaked a bluish lavender on 16 November. Namita woke up earlier than usual and brewed the finest blend of Darjeeling, holding the mug in her hands and dreaming of what the day would bring. Atul and she had agreed at the café that he would come straight from the airport to her apartment. She wouldn't go to the airport to receive him. She would wait for him at home; await the new life with him that she had been longing for.

By early afternoon when the winter sun had disappeared behind the clouds, the doorbell rang and there he was, smiling at her, his sleek black American Tourister by his side.

'I've done it, baby. I am free, I am yours,' he said quietly. Namita ran her slender fingers over his day-old stubble and sharply inhaled the familiar cologne that brought back memories. He looked the same, except perhaps a little leaner. They flung themselves at each other, not in the least bit interested in wasting time on explanations. Three days passed in the greatest bliss Namita had ever known. No more secrets, she thrilled at the thought. *Atul and I belong to each other. Forever.*

And we don't care who knows.

On the fourth day, however, she caught him unawares with a look of despair on his face. And, in that instant, she knew that he hadn't told Renuka, after all. He hadn't been able to and had only been pretending he had for three whole days.

She didn't have to ask him—she just knew. Her voice was strangely calm and controlled when she asked Atul to leave. She was going out, she said, and when she returned, she didn't want any signs of him in the apartment. After two hours, when she turned the key in the door and found that he had really left, she broke down and cried as she never had before. He had taken her to the giddiest heights of ecstasy and dropped her down a cliff. It was over. She had never known such misery in which she didn't want him in her sight and yet wanted him in her arms.

At last taking hold of herself, she plunged even harder into work. The next few months were a whirl of activity with back-to-back projects and countless red eyes to Frankfurt that eventually got her promoted to partner in her company.

One day, en route from the tennis courts at the Gymkhana Club, she happened to run into Atul and Renuka. Her colleagues hadn't exaggerated, Renuka was stunning. Later, Namita would quietly praise herself for being able to carry on a perfectly friendly conversation with them. She also applauded Atul's flawless performance. Never by a word or gesture did he show that they had been anything but business acquaintances.

It wasn't that Namita wasn't aware of her own good looks. There had been several men who admired her and asked her out. While flattered, she never allowed herself to go too far and enter into a serious relationship. Her feelings for Atul had been intense and sincere. She had truly believed he would be hers forever. Damn you, woman, for being so naive, she chided herself.

Her feelings for Atul gradually began to turn into a kind of hate. How could he? The cheat! She wept into her pillow for weeks. His weakness was deplorable. She had been willing to give her life for him and he could not do what he promised he would with every fibre of his being. *Those three days were a lie.* Her cheeks burnt with anger at the thought of his deception. He had even taken off his wedding ring, letting her believe he was free.

Five years went by. Time, the big healer, worked its magic. Namita was now vice-chairman of her company. She looked beautiful with the assurance that success can give a woman. She had a designer apartment, a luxury car, a chauffeur. In her company she was known as a powerful and demanding boss who had not lost her femininity. People adored her. They felt she had a deep, intuitive understanding of their feelings.

One evening, quite unexpectedly, there was a ring at the door. Atul stood there, his suitcase by his side. Namita looked at him with a blank expression. It was like a rerun of an earlier movie. He looked slightly older—he was graying at the temples and had a slight paunch, but this only added to his good looks.

This time Namita realized with a pang that it was for real. Atul had, indeed, left his wife and come back to her. No more pretenses. Such as he was, he was hers. Everything in her heart told her to rush into his arms. The pain of all those years would be washed away with his kisses. Just as she had known the last time around that he had lied, she now knew that Atul had left his family to be with her forever.

His eyes searched hers for signs of acceptance. She could see the love and longing in his eyes. He could see how much she still loved and wanted him.

But as if in slow motion, drawing every ounce of strength from within her, she shut the door. It was the hardest thing she had ever done in her life. Her heart screamed at her to snatch the chance of happiness that was being given to her, that she had longed for all these years

As the door shut on Atul, it seemed to be shutting out her life, as it might have played out in future, in measured seconds. Very deliberately, she turned her back on it. She began to slowly climb the stairs to her room.

From downstairs, the doorbell rang, at first hesitantly, and then with a sense of urgency.

Namita let it ring.

When You Least Expect It

Meera Rajagopalan

'THERE IS no way this is happening,' said Seetharaman as he stormed off.

Subbu wondered why everything with his family had to be so dramatic. It hadn't even been five minutes since his girlfriend, who he thought he'd introduce to his family, had left. Subbu wanted to do this formally—announce his intention to marry her. More than seeking their approval, he wanted to announce this for the sake of formality. The way it is done in civilized families. But clearly, their family didn't fall in that category! On hearing the news, Seetharaman had lost his temper and had just stopped short of flinging things around.

Subbu was aghast. True, he hadn't expected his cross-cultural, unconventional marriage proposal to go down very well, but, still, wasn't this extreme? He was now convinced the father-son relationship was not based on healthy mutual understanding and respect, after all. It seemed like it was all one-way. It was always *he* who had to be the accommodating one. Subbu wagged an angry finger in the air. He was livid. Not anymore, he vowed. I will get my way in this house.

He, too, stormed off to his room and shut the door. Loudly.

None of this would have happened if Subbu hadn't taken the darned bus from Boston to Raleigh, within two weeks of arriving in the US Looking back, he realized he must have looked a sight as he got on the Greyhound bus, with packed Indian snacks in tow. When the driver halted at a service area, Subbu was only too glad to get off the claustrophobic bus and get himself a cup of coffee. Just as he was about to take the styrofoam cup to his lips, someone brushed against him and his coffee spilt on to his shirt.

'Watch where you're go'in,' came a deep, belligerent voice. Subbu looked up to see a huge woman hovering over him, shouting more expletives at the man who had dared to brush against Subbu. She had about fifty paper napkins in her hand, as if by magic. Without waiting for a response, she simply said, 'Here, let me take care of it for you, hon,' and used about half of those to wipe his shirt clean. She then deftly dampened the rest of the stack to clean the shirt, almost spotless.

Subbu, still unused to a strange woman within five feet of him without reason, was embarrassed, and simply looked down at her shocking pink shoes that matched her leotards.

'What, no thanks? Cat got your tongue?' she asked. Subbu, new that he was to the country's ways, wasn't sure if she was serious or joking.

'Thanks,' Subbu mumbled under his breath and finally made bold to look at her face.

He was dazzled by what he saw. Sure, she was huge, but her face had an inexplicable kindness about it that he had only read in books.

'Don't mention it, baby,' she laughed, a full throaty laugh that Subbu was sure could be heard even a mile away.

'Eileen Richards,' she said, and stuck out her hand.

He shook her hand. 'Subbu Koramangala.' He was surprised that his hand fit neatly into hers, and her grip was confident and hard. From where he came from, women had gentler grips.

'Kora what?' she said, and then shook her head. 'Subbu's good nuf.'

Subbu was intuitive enough to notice that she tried to mask her kindness with her loud and abrasive behaviour. He thought her mind was elsewhere, even though she was talking to him. He couldn't help but wonder what her story was. He was hardly used to speaking to women, let alone American women, so he let his curiosity simply slide.

Subbu had just arrived in the US two weeks ago, and was staying at his uncle's house in Boston. He was now going to Raleigh, to North Carolina State University to be specific, and was planning to be there for at least a few months. He hadn't told anyone back home that the uncle had unceremoniously asked him, in just so many words, to leave as soon as was convenient. 'We need the guest room for friends coming from Seattle for the Thanksgiving weekend,' was the explanation Subbu had been given. That was why this bus trip, which was actually proving to be very inconvenient as far as plans go. The bus was taking way too long to get to its destination, and he was starting to feel clammy.

When he got back on the bus, his eyes automatically scanned for Eileen. She was two rows behind him and met his gaze. There was a thin film of water over her large eyes, and Subbu could see she was desperately trying to hold back her tears.

He debated in his head. Surely he wouldn't be a human being if he didn't at least ask her what was wrong, even if he barely knew her. He got up to go to her seat. Then he paused; her voice and larger-than-life demeanour intimidated him. But taking a deep breath, he swiftly walked over to her before he lost his nerve. She looked away, a little embarrassed at her teary state. She didn't want to be caught weeping in front of strangers! The seat next to her was empty, and Subbu took it. Just then the bus began to move. Eileen determinedly looked out of the window, ignoring Subbu seated next to her. Seeing her heavy body heaving with sobs, he understood she was in a bad emotional state.

'Eileen,' Subbu said.

There was no reply.

'Look here,' he spoke in a tone that sounded almost like a command. When she turned to face him, her eyes were red from crying and her mascara all messed up.

Subbu cleared his throat. 'I know it's none of my business, but I can't let someone cry alone. So tell me, what is the matter?'

She gave him a weak smile and looked at him with curiosity. She then, to Subbu's surprise, unburdened herself on him completely. She told him all about her lifelong struggle with drugs, and just when she had started living a normal life after years of therapy, an accident took her daughter away from her. 'My baby really didn't do anything now. Why was she punished when she knew nothin', did nothin'? It was me that should have gone—I was the one with the problems.' She sniffled into her handkerchief.

Subbu was at a loss for words. He felt for her and her situation, but he was terrible at articulating his feelings. So he simply quoted the Bhagavadgita, '"As a person puts on new garments, giving up old ones, the soul similarly accepts new material bodies, giving up the old and useless ones."'

Eileen sat up. 'Wow, it's so beautiful. What does it mean?' she asked, sounding incredulous. Subbu, who was now thankful that his father had made him study some of the Hindu scriptures, launched on a mini version of the Bhagavadgita for the lady. She bowed her head in reverence and listened intently, nodding her head in some places, and frowning in others, as he explained the Hindu concept of atma, death, reincarnation, and immortality.

'Your daughter, surely, will be in a safe place, and will possibly to return to earth soon,' he said with a knowing glance. When she finally looked up at him, Eileen's face radiated an energy that he hoped he had some part in infusing.

She shrugged her broad shoulders. 'Hell, I'm not sure I believe in all this, but what the heck, everything's some form of belief, isn't it?'

Subbu got up to return to his seat.

'This seat isn't taken, you know,' she said, smiling through her tears. Subbu couldn't help but admire her perfectly shaped teeth. He felt heat rising up his cheeks. This woman seemed to have some indefinable charisma about her.

They sat quietly for a while. She then chuckled, 'Thank you for sharing Bhagavadgita's teachings with me.'

'No problem,' he said, and offered her some of the precious chicki he had bought at an Indian store in Boston.

When they arrived in Raleigh, they walked their separate ways. 'See you,' she said, and both knew that that wouldn't happen.

A month later

Subbu still thought about Eileen every now and then and would scan the subways for any signs of her. Her braided hair framing her kind face was something he would never forget, he decided. Even if he had wanted to trace her, it would simply be impossible because he had already forgotten her last name. He Googled her name, and tried the directory, but everything came to nought.

It was exactly a month since his bus trip to Raleigh that it happened again. Then he knew that God, in whatever form, had ordained it. He was at a local Dunkin' Donuts, ordering his usual coffee and jelly doughnut, when he heard a vaguely familiar voice call out loudly, 'Hey!'

He turned to see that it was indeed Eileen, who was at Dunkin' Donuts with a couple of girlfriends. Subbu's happiness was short-lived as it was obvious the euphoric greeting wasn't for him, after all. It was for another man—as tall, dark, and handsome as Subbu had seen in the numerous clothing store flyers, except this man was a bit more portly. Subbu had to admit—Eileen and this man did make a picture-perfect couple, what with matching skin tones and figures! Eileen hugged and kissed the man, before introducing him to her friends. Subbu felt embarrassed, though he wondered if Eileen had seen him at all. He continued with his breakfast by sitting with his back to Eileen's group, occupying an inconspicuous corner table. Just as he bit into his doughnut, he felt a slight thump on his back. He looked up to see a smiling Eileen. Her eyes were now sparkling and bright, a far cry from how she looked on the bus that evening.

'Hi,' she said simply and sat opposite him.

'Hi,' he said, suddenly overcome with shyness.

'How've you been?' Eileen's kind face looked at him with concern.

'Good.'

More silence. He truly didn't know what to say. They sat like that for a few minutes, till the silence got to him. It looked like she would sit like that forever till he spoke.

'How about you?' he finally asked.

'Huh?'

'I mean, how have you been?'

'Good,' she said.

Again, another bout of silence. What he had read on a Snapple cap came to mind. 'On an average, there is a pause in a conversation after every seven minutes.' This was more like every five seconds!

'So what are you up to'" he asked.

She raised an eyebrow just an inch. 'You know, I'm in another job now. Quit the old one—too many bad memories.'

'Oh! Good for you.'

'And what about you?' she said.

He suddenly realized that she did not really know anything about him. 'What do you want to know?'

'I don't know, anything. Everything.'

'We don't have the time for *everything*, you know.' He looked at her slightly amused.

She mock-looked at her non-existent watch. 'Oh, but we do!'

'Well, things are sort of okay with me...' he started, and told her about his life—the university life and the below-the-table gas station work. 'Wow,' Eileen said every now and then.

Suddenly, he stopped, caught his breath and said, 'That's

about it for now.' He felt physically lighter. He thought about how long it had been since he had actually spoken to anyone about his innermost feelings, fears and anxieties. It was liberating talking to Eileen who seemed as non-judgemental as they come. And looking at Eileen, and knowing what all she had battled, his problems seemed too trivial to him.

'That's it?' she asked.

Subbu wasn't sure where he had stopped, and why. He had just wanted to pause to reflect. And thought it was probably not a good thing to get used to a compassionate listener. And he told her so.

'Oh, you poor man,' Eileen said, 'you can get used to talking to me.' She took out a piece of paper and wrote her phone number on it. Subbu had seen so much of exchanged phone numbers in Hollywood movies that he wasn't sure of the subtext. Did this mean 'Call me?' in a husky tone, or simply 'Call me'? The problem was Eileen had a booming voice whose subtle modulations, he simply couldn't understand.

Nervously, he took the paper and folded it into his wallet.

Subbu cleared his throat. 'You probably have to go back to your…um…friend over there.'

Eileen looked in the direction Subbu was looking. The man she had greeted earlier was seated two tables away, sipping his coffee.

'Oh, that man?' Eileen pointed her thumb at the man. 'He's a cousin and I wanted him to meet one of my girlfriends. You know…trying to hook them up and all. This meet up was sort of a set-up,' she added conspiratorially.

Subbu's shoulders slumped with relief.

'So, what now?' Eileen asked, looking at him with her large limpid eyes.

'Well,' he replied, a silly grin plastered on his face, 'I'm glad I saw you here.'

'Me too, hon,' she said.

Then she slowly got up. 'See you around,' This time it felt like they would.

Back in the apartment, he could not get a minute to himself. When he did get some free time the next morning, he took out his wallet and checked the number. He turned the scrap of paper over in his hand several times. He felt like calling her, but what would he say? Would it even be appropriate? What would his family think? Would it lead anywhere? And finally, why was he worrying about it so much?

He simply folded the paper and put it back in his wallet. He muttered to himself, 'If it is to happen, it will. God, give me one sign that I should call, and I will.'

Unsure what form the sign would take (it was God after all, and he was prone to cryptic signs), Subbu eagerly tried to convert every single happening in his life into a positive sign. Did he get a bus immediately? That surely meant that he must get in touch with the person he met on the bus! Did he see a large woman with a beautiful smile in a Dunkin' Donuts? Surely, God meant for that to be a sign. And so it went, though no sign, however pertinent, could drive him to make that phone call.

As days flew by, he became even more hesitant to call her. But he never stopped wondering: *What if?*

Three Years Later

Subbu was back on the same route—Boston to Raleigh. Only

this time, he was flying. He had just boarded the plane, paranoid and alert to get on the plane first, lest it leave without him. Despite his years in America, he was still timid about adapting to this country's culture that demanded everything should be fast: food, travel and relationships. Again, his thoughts wandered to Eileen. She was something else. Back in India, at least in his family, he was used to women either being submissive, like his mother was, or totally dominating, like some of his aunts. But there was always an attempt at projecting an image of perfection which made it very difficult to share his life with anyone and be himself, the way he was. His fears and his imperfections had to be his alone. For the first time, Eileen—kind, portly and almost masculine as they come—showed him that it was okay to let your warts show. Subbu sighed as he put on his seat belt. Three years, and he still remembered her. He had no clue where she was; perhaps she was married again? Wherever she was, he told himself, he hoped she was happy. Surely, she deserved it.

Just then, there was some commotion in the front of the aisle. 'Sorry, ma'am,' said the stewardess, as she stepped out of the way of a slightly large woman. Subbu had just peeked out of his seat to see what the fuss was about, and he literally felt his heart stop. *It was Eileen.* She looked a bit older, but the kindness on her face was intact.

Subbu wanted to wave her over, but was suddenly attacked by a bout of intense shyness. From the corner of his eye he could sense her approaching his seat, but he pretended to read a magazine. He buried his face further in the magazine, not daring to look up. The familiar booming voice he had come to admire, now said, 'Excuse me, sir, this is my seat.'

No one could possibly mistake this sign, Subbu mused. Is this your sign, God? he asked. But aren't you sending it a bit too late? Finally, Subbu resurfaced from the magazine and looked up at Eileen.

She shrieked, 'It's *you*. You do have a habit of following me everywhere, Subbu.'

'Yes,' Subbu said sheepishly and smiled broadly.

Someone dared to clear his throat behind Eileen and she simply darted a menacing look at him, which immediately shut him up. But she moved as if to make way for the fellow passenger, not that there was room enough for him to pass through the narrow aisle. Eileen cocked an eyebrow at Subbu. He blinked. It took him a moment to understand that he needed to shift to the window seat.

'Sorry,' he said and made way for Eileen to sit in the seat he had warmed for so long.

The pilot's voice filled the plane. The plane was getting ready to take off; instructions were given to the flight attendants to lock the doors. When the lights were dimmed for take off, Subbu turned slightly to look at his co-passenger.

'Eileen,' he said.

'Mmm...hmm...You remember my name?'

'Of course, like you remember mine,' he said quietly. He sent a silent prayer before taking the plunge. 'I have thought about you nearly every day for the past three years.'

As soon as the words were out of his mouth, he regretted them. Perhaps this confession should have come at the end of the flight. What if she took offence? What if she were married? It was going to be a very unpleasant flight, he decided.

'Why didn't you just call?' she asked.

'A sign.'

'What?'

'I was waiting for a sign.'

'What, like a traffic light?'

'No, something from above.'

'The only thing that comes from above spontaneously is crow shit, brother,' she said and laughed at her own joke.

Subbu was not amused. 'Well, this is a sign, isn't it?' he asked in a businesslike tone.

'What this is is a goddamn plane.'

'Well, both of us being on the same plane...it's...it's got to mean something.'

Eileen chuckled. 'Oh, it means something, all right. It means you have way too much time on your hands.'

Subbu closed his eyes. This was not going as he had expected. Oh well, he surmised. What did he expect? That she would have pined for him all these years and waited for a strange man from a strange land? *You naive idiot, what were you thinking?*

He picked up his magazine again when he felt her arm on his. 'So, tell me what you've been doing, Subbu.' Her tone was gentle this time.

Subbu launched into an explanation of his recent trip to India. He bemoaned the fact that his cousins had cheated his family of their ancestral property because of which he was compelled to come to the US to eke out a living. He was here, he explained, because even at the lowest end, life was better for him here.

Eileen smiled, 'You look good, Subbu, you must be doing well here.'

'Not so great, but pulling along. Enough about me; what are you up to these days?'

'Hmm...let me see. Where did we leave off at Dunkin' Donuts?'

'You were telling me about the new job you had got...' said Subbu.

'Gosh, you remember!' Eileen looked surprised. 'You know what, I never expected that job to last, but it has, and I am now their regional manager.'

Subbu nodded appreciatively. 'Sometimes, things turn out differently than you imagine. Things you believe will work don't, and things you believe will fail, turn out superbly.'

Eileen mock clapped. 'What about your life otherwise, Subbu?' she asked him suddenly.

He paused, the significance of her question sinking in.

'I have no life otherwise, Eileen. Truly. How about you?' There, he had asked her the question, the answer to which he most dreaded.

'Nothing happening on that, nothing worth mentioning anyway,' she laughed.

Subbu's spirits soared. He looked at her again, a silly grin spreading on his face. 'You mean...'

'Signs. I had to know too, you know. I had given myself until the end of this year to see if I would run into you. I'm a sucker for signs myself.'

They spent the rest of the flight holding hands.

And now, nearly a year later, he desperately wanted to propose to the woman he loved—in fact, the only woman he had truly loved. But it was the family that was stopping him from being happy. Was it because she was Black? Or because she was three years older than him? Or was it because they thought that their tight-knit Indian community would look down upon them? Wasn't his happiness more important than anything else?

Subbu tapped the ring in his pocket and went to bed. Tomorrow, he would propose to the love of his life, come what may.

He had left behind everything he had in India to move to the US to be with his son and his daughter-in-law, both professors at the North Carolina State University at Raleigh. And here they were, trying to stop his happiness. He had sacrificed so much for his son and daughter in the sixty-five years of his existence. Why, he had even lived with his shrew of a wife for Seetharaman's sake. Subbu had no fond memories of his marriage; he and his wife never got along till she died five years ago. He had endured that life only for the sake of his children. Now, it was time for his life to begin.

Urmila

Sudha Subramanian

꧁꧂

'MY LADY! My lady!' Krithika called out to Urmila who lay fast asleep, swathed between silk bed sheets covered with rich brocade work. The faithful and chirpy Krithika was Urmila's best friend. In all these fourteen years, whenever Urmila would drift in and out of sleep, it was Krithika who stayed put long nights, on the ready to attend to Urmila's needs.

Today, Krithika had prepared an elaborate beauty bath for Urmila and was now desperate to wake her up. It was, after all, a momentous occasion, long-awaited by Urmila! It was a beautiful morning in Ayodhya. The first rays of the sun brought with it a new era of hope to everyone in the kingdom. The soft golden rays danced merrily in Urmila's room. A cool breeze entered through the open windows. Beautifully carved gemstones on the walls sparkled lustrously, as if to join in the festive spirit that prevailed everywhere.

Contrary to what Krithika assumed, Urmila, the other beautiful daughter of Janaka, the younger sister of Sita, and the wife of Lakshmana, was wide awake. How could she sleep when her beloved was coming home? Had the gruelling fourteen years come to an end or was she dreaming? It was clear from Krithika's beaming face that her ordeal was about to end. Sometimes it was hard to believe that fate had cruelly separated her lord from her for so many years. Urmila sighed. She also yearned to be reunited with her elder sister, the beautiful and noble, Sita. Memories of a happy childhood spent with Sita flitted through Urmila's mind. She remembered the time when she and Sita played with dolls and ran around aimlessly in the palace garden, their golden anklets creating a melody of their own.

Suddenly, she felt overwhelmed with emotion. She recalled her final meeting with her dear lord before he left her for fourteen years. She had replayed the moment so many times in her memory that she could recall the meeting in astonishing detail. Urmila sat up in her elaborately carved four-poster bed. Her lips were quivering and her weary eyes could shed no more tears—albeit of joy today—because she had cried enough all these years.

Urmila's glance fell on the sari, hanging from a hook on the wall. It was a beautiful golden yellow sari, with a deep red border. Little white pearls were tucked elegantly along the red brocade and small trinkets that were laced along the pallu, chimed softly in the wind. Only she and Krithika knew the significance of this sari—it had been carefully preserved by Urmila all these years, for it held Lakshmana's warm embrace. It was the same sari that had taken Lakshmana's tears and his caress. For many nights, Urmila had slept with the sari next to her. She had never allowed anyone to touch it or wash it because, she believed, it carried Lakshmana's smell in its folds. The sari was her mirror image—breathtakingly beautiful, but lonely and sad.

Urmila turned her head and saw the bright rays of the sun enter her room. A gentle smile spread on her face when she wondered about her life. She had had a strange love story. It was the story of a woman who loved her man immensely, but barely got to know him before they were forced to live apart. Of course Urmila had, over the years, come to know him through other people—the palace attendants and the older members of the public who had doted on him as a kid, but there was still a void in her to find out for herself what her husband was all about. Despite her unfamiliarity with Lakshmana, Urmila loved him with utter devotion.

She suddenly remembered Krithika's presence in the room. 'What is it, dear friend?' asked Urmila, languidly running her bejewelled fingers through her long, lustrous hair.

Krithika could barely contain her excitement. 'Well, my beautiful Lady, the auspicious hour has arrived! I just heard from the guards that the party has reached the outskirts of Ayodhya. Your dear sister, Lord Rama and your husband are being welcomed by the people of the kingdom. In fact, Queen Kaikeyi has specially ordered that the entire palace be decorated with roses,' Krithika gushed.

Urmila couldn't contain her excitement either. She jumped out of her bed and stood for a split second—what was she going to do first? She walked up to the sari on the wall and gingerly ran her fingers along the silk brocade. She brought it to her lips. *My lord.* Remembering she had to get ready, she rushed to catch a quick glimpse of herself in the mirror, when a sudden shiver ran through her body. 'Will I recognize him? Will he recognize me?' But she knew that even if her eyes deceived her, her heart would lead her to him.

Krithika carried on, 'Royal Princess, I cannot bear to see

your tragic eyes any more. They have shed tears in sleep and when awake. It is time for you to smile again...' her voice trailed and then she burst into tears.

Urmila smiled at Krithika indulgently. She knew her friend so well. Urmila often wondered if Krithika's married life had suffered because of her. Krithika's tears moved her. Urmila felt she had found a sister in her—so devout and kind that she wasn't sure if she truly deserved that kind of loyalty and affection.

'Krithika,' Urmila said firmly, trying to rein in her emotions. 'I think you should also go back to your house and rest. Now that my lord is back, you deserve some rest, too. You have been such a pillar of strength for me all these years...' she managed, before breaking down.

Far from the palace, in the outskirts of Ayodhya, throngs of people had gathered, just to catch a glimpse of their beloved Crown Prince, Rama, who was returning, after vanquishing, from what they had heard, the human incarnation of evil itself. As Rama approached the city with Sita and Lakshmana, he had no choice but to step down from the extravagantly-decorated chariot that his brother, Bharata, had specially dispatched to him. Rama decided to walk to his home, meeting and greeting as many people as possible. Sita and Lakshmana followed suit.

Back in the palace, Urmila stood near the window, watching the festivities. The streets were decorated with colourful rangolis; floral garlands hung over the doorsteps; women and children, dressed in festive finery, thronged the streets. At one corner she saw a group of men and women dancing and singing in a giant circle with dholaks. In the palace, Krithika and Urmila's other girlfriends sang loudly as they got busy changing the curtains and polishing the silverware. As she looked out, Urmila watched a mother scold her child for smudging the colourful rangoli with his chubby fingers. Being a princess, Urmila had almost forgotten how life was for a commoner. When the mother reprimanded the child every time he erased the rangoli, Urmila felt a sudden pang of envy settle on her. She longed to lead a normal life like this woman: a husband, with whom she could share her life, and children whom she could dote on; instead of remaining cloistered in the palace and imagining how life would be as a wife or a mother. At times, she found even the misunderstandings among couples that her married women friends knowledgeably spoke of, very charming because, she realized, the thrill lay in making up after a tiff. Urmila could no longer wait for such a life, filled with exciting possibilities—of love, passion, lovers' tiffs, and then the unmatched joy of making up with her husband.

Urmila looked again at the sari, feeling weak in the knees, anticipating her reunion with her lord. Just then she saw her mother-in-law, the ever elegant Sumitra, walk into her chamber carrying a large silver plate covered with a red silk cloth. She was followed by her two close maids-in-waiting whom Urmila recognized as Ashwini and Ratna. They also were carrying plates covered with silk cloths. Urmila affectionately regarded her mother-in-law's greying hair and her tired eyes that now held a sense of relief. It suddenly dawned on Urmila that in all these years, she had hardly spent any time with her mother-in-law.

Urmila ran to Sumitra, fell into her arms, and drowned her tears into her mother-in-law's bosom. The two women held each other for a long time, overcome as they were with emotion. They didn't speak a word, but their relief and joy was palpable on their glowing faces. The room fell silent and the mood was emotionally charged for everyone.

Sumitra and Urmila sat on the ornate bed. Sumitra cupped Urmila's beautiful face in her hands and smiled, 'My darling, you deserve a beautiful life,' she said. 'Your suffering has come to an end. Your devotion snatched my son from the jaws of death and your sacrifice helped him kill the strongest of asuras. You have made us all proud.' Urmila, as befitting a royal daughter-in-law, looked away bashfully. She silently wondered if she deserved her mother-in-law's generous praise. While she was proud that her husband had helped a great deal in rescuing her sister, Sita, from the clutches of the asura king, Ravana, Urmila sometimes felt guilty that it was Lakshmana who had unwittingly enabled in Sita's kidnapping. He was partly responsible for Sita's misery. Urmila sighed heavily, relieved that things had turned out well in the end. Her eyes fell on the silver plate her mother-in-law had now placed on the table. Sumitra took off the red silk cloth that covered the plate.

Urmila stared at the beautiful brocade red sari. 'What is this, Mother?' she asked, feeling the soft silk under her fingers.

Sumitra smiled. 'A special sari made by the royal designer— just for you! I would like you to wear it today.' The sari sparkled in the sunrays that filtered in through the windows. All the women in the room slowly gathered around the sari to take a better look. They gasped audibly, stunned by the sheer beauty of the fabric and design. Urmila smiled politely, eager to head out to greet her husband, brother-in-law and sister. She didn't want to waste further time on her wardrobe.

'I know, what you are thinking, daughter,' Sumitra smiled, 'but I insist you wear this. This sari was kept in the puja and has the blessings of Shakti. Wear this when you welcome Rama, the

Lord of Ayodhya, the man who rules our hearts.' She touched Urmila's face and held her hand for a few seconds, praying for her daughter-in-law's happiness. She had many other things to attend to before her children—Rama, Lakshmana and Sita—got home. Her next stop would be at the royal kitchen to personally supervise the preparation of the day's feast. Urmila bent down and touched Sumitra's feet. Sumitra blessed her with a warm kiss on the forehead.

A smile escaped Urmila's lips as she watched her mother-in-law and the two women leave. She looked at Krithika and suddenly realized that the room was filled with excitement. Sumitra had got everyone not just clothes, but also some fine jewellery and sweets. An exuberant Krithika pulled Urmila into the garden and ran near the fountains. She held out her hands to Urmila and the two women giggled and danced in circles, their faces upturned at the skies. Soon, their other friends joined them in the garden: Asha, Brinda, Neelanjana and Mythri. All of them laughed and danced joyously. Tears of joy prickled Urmila's eyelids. It had been so long since she had had so much fun!

Urmila danced till she was dizzy and sat on the grass, gasping for breath. Just then her maid-in-waiting, Brinda, walked in. Brinda did a small curtsy and announced that things were ready for Urmila's bath. Krithika opened up Urmila's long tresses and started applying oil on them.

'How do you think my sister will be, Krithika?' asked Urmila. 'She must be very weak after all that she has been through...'

'My Lady!' Krithika said, 'I have heard that she still looks radiant after all these years of difficulties. She is a bit weak, but is otherwise glowing with relief and happiness.'

Urmila nodded and quietly wondered if her friend knew anything about her beloved lord, too. Krithika smiled, not disclosing what else she may have heard from others about the two royal brothers who were returning home to Ayodhya today. 'A tub full of warm water and rose petals has been prepared, dear Lady. We should go now,' was all she said.

Urmila didn't probe any further. She decided to be patient and wait to see her husband herself. For the first time in all these years, a tinge of pink coloured her cheeks. She quickly looked away from Krithika, not wanting to be caught blushing like a new bride! She certainly didn't want her friend to tease her like old times. The last time Krithika had teased her had been on the day of the exile.

Urmila had vivid recollections of that fateful morning. It was on that day that she had insisted on keeping her long tresses open like how Lakshmana liked it. When Krithika had insisted on braiding it, Urmila had playfully shoved her away. Krithika had been in a relentlessly teasing mood. 'My Lady, you have to tell me why you don't want me to braid your hair. Is it because someone likes it better with your hair left open?' she giggled, Urmila's other girlfriends joining in the mirth.

Urmila pulled a face. '*I* like my hair like this, any problem?' she cocked an eyebrow at Krithika.

'But I thought you hate your hair falling on your face?' Krithika retorted with a fresh fit of giggles. Just then Lakhsmana walked into Urmila's chamber and Krithika and her friends left the room unobtrusively.

Lakshmana had looked disturbed. How could he tell the lady whom he loved so deeply, that he was leaving for the forest and would not see her for a long time? Urmila, even though a new bride, intuitively caught on to her husband's pensive mood. Lakshmana ran his hand over Urmila's hair and kissed her on the forehead. 'You look so beautiful, beloved,' he said in a melancholic tone, wondering when again he would get to say that. Urmila blushed, but sensed something was amiss. Lakshmana looked deep into her eyes, tugging at Urmila's heartstrings—she loved him so much that she could spend an eternity just standing like that with the love of her life by her side. After a long time, Lakshmana asked in a choked voice, 'Urmi, my dear, do you love me?'

She glanced away shyly. Who wouldn't love this man—someone so handsome, a man of character, and highly principled?

'I do,' Urmila finally whispered. 'Don't you know that?'

At that moment, Lakshmana brought her to his bosom and hugged her so tight that she could barely breathe. He gently released her and told her about the vanavas, the exile that his brother, Rama, and Urmila's sister, Sita, were embarking upon.

'I am going with them to the forest for fourteen years, my love,' he said, not looking her in the eye. Urmila pushed him away, feeling confused, shattered and angered, all at once. Her husband's loyalty towards his eldest brother was legendary, but what about to her, his wife? While she battled her conflicting emotions—to feel proud of her husband or to hold him back selfishly—she realized that Lakshmana was slowly taking off his royal clothes and putting on saffron-hued ascetic robes.

Urmila was certainly not liking the speed at which things were happening! She ran to him and wanted to stop him, hold him back before it was too late. But before she could do anything, Lakshmana embraced her and kissed her passionately.

He then whispered, 'I love you with all my heart, Urmi. Trust me and wait for me. I have to do this but I will come back one day.'

Urmila felt faint. She wanted to tell him so many things, unspoken words that were now jumbled up in her tongue. She wished he could read her mind and her heart. She wanted him to know how Krithika had found out through the palace grapevine that she and Lakshmana had met secretly in Mithila before they got married. Urmila had wanted to share this and other secrets, big and small, with Lakshmana; but here he was, biding her goodbye for fourteen years! She just couldn't believe this was happening to her. As her heart raced and tears streamed down her cheeks, she felt a lone tear land on her hand. She looked up and saw Lakshmana wipe his own moist eyes. Before she could react, she felt his lips on hers. They shared a long passionate kiss before Lakshmana tore himself away from her and walked through the open doors that led to the palace corridors, without looking back even once.

Urmila had stood there for an entire hour, feeling utterly helpless. She had shut the door and vowed then that she would open it only for her lord when he is back.

Now, after all these years, as Urmila closed her eyes, she felt a strange warmth settle on her. She played with the rose petals in the bath and applied the fragrance powder on her face.

'My Lady, it is getting late!' Krithika's excited voice interrupted Urmila's reverie. Urmila emerged out of the warm waters of the bath, energized and relaxed. Krithika laid out on the bed the clothes and jewellery Sumitra had brought for her daughter-in-law. As all the maids-in-waiting helped Urmila get dressed, a glow of happiness shone on her face. Krithika brushed Urmila's long tresses and left them open—just the way Lakshmana liked it.

When Urmila was ready, Krithika sent out a silent prayer thanking God for the ordeal that had finally ended. Urmila was looking resplendent in the beautiful red sari. The golden jhumkas that danced wildly in her ears, complemented her ringing laughter. The dark kohl made her eyes sparkle so much that she looked absolutely divine. Krithika couldn't help but wipe some kohl from the corner of her own eye and place it as a dot on Urmila's chin. 'This will take care of the evil eye,' she declared to an amused Urmila.

Urmila had just one last thing to do before welcoming her husband. She still had to decorate the door that had remained closed all these years. She ordered for the finest flowers from the palace garden and began her decoration, when she heard the drumbeats. She heard the laughter of children and people cheering. She got back to decorating the door with a smile. She had to ensure the door looked perfect when her husband entered through it. The cheering and the music got louder now. Unable to contain her curiosity, she turned and noticed all her girlfriends glued to the windows. They murmured excitedly. Suddenly, Krithika cried, 'They are here! They are here!'

Urmila didn't rush to the windows. She suddenly craved for some privacy, wanting to rein in her rising sense of excitement before meeting her husband. At that moment, Krithika screamed, 'My Lady! Look who is here…' Urmila dropped all her inhibitions and ran towards the window.

At first it wasn't clear; a cloud of dust eclipsed her lord. Then slowly, her brother-in-law came in her line of vision—dignified and genuinely happy to be home, smiling at the people of Ayodhya, still dressed in austere clothes. Urmila spotted her beautiful sister, Sita, on one side of Rama. Urmila sucked in her breath. There he was, her lord, on the other side of his brother, looking as handsome and attractive as ever. Urmila's eyes gave way to a flood of tears and her heart pounded wildly. When Lakshmana looked up and met her gaze, it was as if the whole world had come to a standstill. In that brief moment they were reunited, man and wife, before the crowd surged forward and mobbed the heroes.

Urmila drew in a sharp breath. There was just one thing left to be done. She pushed herself away from the window and laughing through tears, ran to the elaborately decorated door and opened it for the first time in fourteen years.

Blossoms

Roshan Radhakrishnan

$\mathcal{I}$T WAS now or never.

He looked around him one last time to make sure no one else was around. The halls were empty but he knew that the scenario could change any moment. It wasn't the hallway, though that too frightened him. The main source of his trepidation lay at either end of the corridor, of course.

From the half open doorway of the staff room in front of him, he could hear Mrs Prathibha Devi talking about something that had happened in class that day. She was regaling a colleague about how she had caught a student dozing in her classroom. Even though Prashant couldn't see her from where he stood, his teacher's description of how she dealt with the boy was vivid enough to give him the shivers. It made him visualize the documentary images of a ferocious tiger, toying with a helpless deer. On any given day, her loud voice was frightening enough, but today it warned him of her undisputed position within the staff room.

The other end of the corridor offered him a fair view of

the proceedings inside the biology lab. The students all stood with their backs to him. Their focus was around a solitary microscope as Mrs Ruchika Purushotham, in her stentorian voice, described the differences between a dicot and a monocot. The students seemed to be engrossed in what she was saying.

Behind Prashant, the physics lab's door was half ajar. He had just stepped out of it to attend to something urgent. And therein lay the element of luck he so desperately needed now. He couldn't keep an eye on all three doors simultaneously. He'd just have to take the risk that no one would come out for the next thirty seconds. He took a deep breath before bending down on one knee.

He was conscious of his own school bag as he lifted it. Usually, it would have been heavy, packed with his bulky textbooks, but today, even without them, he found the bag weighing down on him. He glanced back and forth one last time, making sure no one was coming from any of the rooms, and then reached forward. Even though there were a dozen student backpacks lying on the floor beside the Physics lab, he knew exactly which one he wanted. He had seen the black bag every day for months now, committing to memory the broken zip on top and the brand name that had now faded over time. He knew the bag, all right, and could have identified it from a hundred other bags, if necessary.

Then he zipped open his own bag and removed the contents, neatly wrapped in yesterday's newspaper. He unfolded the paper carefully and stared at what lay within. He debated whether to remove the plastic cover that held it all together at the bottom. It was tacky, but necessary to avoid everything falling apart and becoming a mess. He'd just picked up the first plastic bag he'd found at home which suited his needs. In hindsight, he wished he'd wrapped it up in a better cover, maybe some gift wrapping paper. She would have liked that.

A chair screeched in the staff room, jerking him back to the present. Mrs Prathibha Devi had got up from her seat. Prashant froze; he could not afford to get caught! He quickly placed the package he was holding in the black bag, zipping it up before Mrs Prathibha Devi walked out of the staff room.

But nothing happened. He heard her animated chatter spill out of the room, now about a girl whose industrialist father was donating a large sum of money for the school's sports complex that was coming up next year. With a silent prayer of gratitude on his lips, he turned around and hurried back to the physics lab. He stood at the doorway, resolutely not making eye contact with any of his classmates who were engrossed in filling their record books.

'Ma'am, may I please come in?' he asked politely.

'Yes, come in,' said Mrs Chandana Gowda, without looking up from the textbook she was reading.

By lunch break, everyone in his class knew about the gift. Triveni was suddenly the centre of attraction of all the girls. The contents of her school bag was the only topic of discussion on everyone's lips, Prashant noted with amusement while eating his lunch quietly. He tried to see her face and gauge her reaction, but she was busy getting her leg pulled by her friends. He decided not to attract attention to himself by modifying his normal routine and, hence, got up and nonchalantly left the classroom after finishing his lunch. He went for a walk along the school corridors to kill time till the bell signalled the end of the lunch hour.

He remembered the trepidation with which he'd bought the flowers from the shop near his housing society, looking back over his shoulder repeatedly to make sure he wasn't spotted by anyone he knew. What would he have said if a neighbour—any of those nosy uncles and aunties—had found him buying the most resplendent roses? What is a fifteen-year-old boy doing in a flower shop? Shouldn't he be studying? These would have been the questions they would have tossed around in their mind before informing his parents. Prashant swallowed hard, feeling a thin film of sweat settle on his upper lip.

There would have been no way he could have explained the flowers had he come across anyone on the way back home from the flower shop. The only option had been to keep them inside his school bag and carry the dozen odd books in his arms. He had deliberately delayed entering his home that evening. He waited for his mother to go upstairs for lighting the lamps in the prayer room, before entering the house and making a dash for his room. The rest of the evening had been spent waiting patiently for the mundane chore of dinner and small talk with his parents and brother to end so that he could go back to his room...and breathe the heady fragrance of the flowers.

Prashant sat on a bench near the canteen and examined his fingers with a wistful smile. They were still sore from where the thorns had pricked them. Last night after dinner, he had meticulously scrapped off all the thorns from the long stems so they wouldn't hurt her. She probably would never notice, but that was okay. She was worth every drop of blood that had appeared on his fingers.

'Prashant! Prashant! Stop!'

He turned around, startled at the sound of his name, then relaxed. It was Seema, his classmate, coming back from the canteen. She was one of the few girls in class he felt comfortable talking to. Of course, that had more to do with the fact that she was a family friend's daughter than anything else, he supposed. She slowed down as she reached him, looking a little breathless from the brisk walking in the afternoon sun.

'Did you hear about Triveni?' she asked, her pert nose flaring with excitement. Seema was cute: curly hair that framed her oval face; bright, thick-lashed eyes, and a button nose that Prashant thought made her look like a doll.

Prashant assumed a neutral tone, 'I saw all the girls surrounding her, but I have no idea what's going on. Why? What happened?' He wondered if Seema could hear his wildly beating heart.

'Oh my God! It was awesome, man,' said Seema. 'After today's Physics practicals, Triveni came out and found these gorgeous roses in her bag. A whole bunch of them—red, orange, yellow and even a couple of blue ones.'

'Really? Roses? Wow. Who gave it?' Prashant wondered if he should enroll in the after school theatre class.

Seema waved her hands in the air. 'Oho, that's the best part, yaar. There was a card attached to the bouquet.' She allowed herself a small sigh and asked, 'Can you guess what it said?'

He could rattle off the card's message in his sleep. 'No, how will I know, silly? Tell me.'

Seema gesticulated with her skinny arms and said in a sing-song voice: 'It said: "Sometimes, a simple gesture from someone can brighten our day and they don't even know it. I just wanted you to know that your smile brightens my day... every day. Happy Valentine's Day." So romantic, na? The guy didn't even sign his name, can you imagine?'

'Hmm...good for her,' said Prashant.

Seema continued, 'The girls are all still sitting in the classroom, trying to identify him by the handwriting. We think it could be Riyaz, Ben or Roshan. Only one of these guys would do such a thing.'

Prashant sat up. 'But don't you think Riyaz would have told Triveni directly? He is bold enough to even propose to Katrina Kaif!'

Seema nodded, 'Hmm...that's also true. He isn't the type to play these sort of games, right? Last year, remember, he gave Sheena chocolates on Valentine's Day? God knows, let's see who it turns out to be.'

'Anyway, what was Triveni's reaction? Is she embarrassed or pissed?' Prashant's heart raced, nervous about what Seema would say. He had not been able to get a good glimpse of Triveni before leaving for his lunch break stroll.

'Pissed?!' Seema cried incredulously. 'Wow. You really don't know anything about girls, do you? Are you kidding me? Go see for yourself. She's blushing like a bride over there. She's such a fair cutie-pie anyway and now, with everyone ragging her and all, she really looks like a strawberry milkshake. I swear I've never seen her so happy, Prashant—'

The loud ringing of the bell interrupted her mid-sentence.

'Damn the bell,' Seema continued, once the ringing had stopped. 'Come on, we'll be late for class.' She mock-shivered. 'Next is Tiger Devi, isn't it?'

'Yes, it is. You go on, Seema, I'll join you in a minute.' Prashant grinned broadly once Seema had disappeared into the school building. *Triveni was blushing like a bride*. He high-fived the air.

He'd done it! He'd made the most beautiful girl in their entire batch smile today. So what if Triveni would never know it was him? The plan had anyway been to let her know she was loved. There was nothing more to it. He took a deep breath and tried unsuccessfully to compose himself as he walked back to his classroom.

He was surprised that the ragging had still not stopped. He inconspicuously walked past Triveni's desk to his table at the back of the room. He watched her giggle as her best friends teased her and she tried to stop them from pulling the flowers out of her bag for all to see. He felt at peace as he opened his textbook. Everything had gone according to plan. 'Happy Valentine's Day, Triveni,' he said in a low voice, muted further by the cacophony that prevailed.

Triveni sat on her bed, staring at the flowers she'd snuck up into her room after school. Her parents may not have appreciated the fact that their daughter had secret admirers sending her flowers.

Triveni had suffered a few anxious minutes as she entered the house, worried that her mother would spot the extra bulge in her bag and, somehow, magically know about the scandalous secret it contained. Luckily, her mother's eyes were now trained on Ruby, their pet terrier, who had chosen that exact moment to chase the neighbourhood cat across the yard and, thus, distract Amma while Triveni made a dash to her room. She made a mental note to give Ruby an extra treat under the table tomorrow morning at breakfast.

Triveni sighed. The day may have ended, but the mystery remained. Trust Namitha and Priya to find cryptic clues where

Holmes and Poirot would have long given up. The number of flowers, the number of each colour, the significance of every colour of rose: to her friends, each and everything about the surprise bouquet was a vital clue in discovering the name of the sender. And then there was the note, of course.

She stared at the note again, trying to decipher who her mystery Valentine was. Priya and Namitha felt it had to be either Ben or Riyaz. They had actually gone up to the boys and asked them directly, but both had vociferously denied it. That clown, Roshan, had instantly owned up, but a few simple questions were enough to understand that he was bluffing, as usual. Triveni's curiosity was killing her. The fact of the matter was that when the final bell rang and they all scrambled into the school bus, she was no closer to identifying the person than when she first discovered the gorgeous flowers in her school bag.

For the umpteenth time, she picked up the note and read the words, trying to decipher its meaning. She looked up and caught her reflection in the mirror. She was still smiling and that made it seven hours at a stretch!

But it was only natural she would blush so much. This was her first Valentine's gift, making her the envy of all her friends. That was not the only reason for her happiness, of course. She couldn't help smiling because the gesture behind the act made her feel special and loved and...and beautiful.

Triveni had borrowed a vase, which was lying idle in her younger sister's room, and placed it on her own dressing table. She now filled it with water and then took out the immaculate roses from her bag. She placed them carefully into the vase, one rose at a time. She suddenly realized the stems were soft to the touch. On careful observation, it appeared as if the sender had taken the trouble to remove the thorns so she would not prick her fingers. *Nice.*

Triveni hummed a Hindi film song tune and spent some time in arranging the roses to her satisfaction. This proved rather challenging as the vibrant colours teased and coaxed her to try different arrangements each time she thought she had nailed the perfect presentation.

A good ten minutes later, she finally gave up and fell back on to her bed, frustrated. She decided to pack her school bag to prepare for the following morning. As she rummaged through the backpack, taking out the petals and the plastic bag the bouquet had come wrapped in, she saw a piece of damp paper stuck to the bottom of the bag. She was about to aim it at the dustbin when something caught her eye. She stared at the paper for what seemed like an eternity. She found herself smiling again; she couldn't help it.

It was now or never; she had to do it.

Triveni had been willing herself to hold Mrs Sharnisha Faisal's gaze as the bespectacled lady droned on about Pythagoras Theorem and the geometric wonder that linked two sides of a triangle to the third. Triveni nodded sagely whenever the teacher's gaze fell on her. But she was barely paying attention today, the words and diagrams weren't registering in her mind.

She wiped her clammy palm in her floral handkerchief that was embroidered with two intertwined blossoming roses. Of all things, she muttered to herself, feeling hot in her cheeks.

Namitha, sitting beside her, looked at her and tapped her watch. 'When?' the gesture asked.

Triveni took a deep breath and exhaled in one sharp release.

'Now,' she hissed into Namitha's ear.

Triveni took out the small neatly folded piece of paper from her pencil case and handed the chit to Namitha, whose hands closed over the chit.

Namitha brought her hand to the edge of her desk while Mrs Faisal turned to demonstrate the magic of Pythagoras with new numbers. A hand reached out and silently took the chit from Namitha. Seema, who now had the chit, took a quick peek at the name on the paper. She almost squealed and passed it on to the industrious Nithila, who quickly passed it on to her neighbour without bothering to steal a look herself.

The graceful ballet of silently passing the chit from one end of the classroom to the other had begun.

A few minutes before the class ended, it was Renjith's turn to pass on the chit to his neighbour, Prashant. Prashant looked up, a trifle annoyed to be disturbed just when he was busy filling little hearts in the triangles he had drawn on his notebook. He took the chit from Renjith and was about to pass it to the boy on the other side of him, when his eyes caught the name on the chit.

Prashant.

He nudged Renjith and gesticulated, 'Who gave this?'

Renjith shook his head, 'No idea.'

A few minutes later, unaware of the little drama unfolding right in front of her, Mrs Faisal finally ended her duel with the triangles and settled her heavy bottom on the chair to take attendance. The classroom hummed with the sound of textbooks being closed and the chattering of students. Prashant finally gathered the courage to take out the chit he had tucked into his notebook.

He was a bit confused. He had always been a part of the

delivery service but never a recipient of any secret chit that tantalized his senses. He looked up one final time to make sure the teacher was suitably preoccupied, before turning his complete attention to the chit.

His eyebrows shot up at what was written on the paper. 'What the f...' almost slipped out of his mouth.

Renjith wiggled his eyebrows at Prashant. *What is it, man?*

Prashant shook his head, feeling puzzled.

What was the laundry receipt of his dad's business suit doing in school? More importantly, why on earth was there a heart drawn on the top in shiny pink ink?

He looked up and found three pairs of eyes looking at him with amusement. Priya and Namitha started giggling softly, covering their mouths to escape Mrs Faisal's wrath.

And the third pair of eyes, the most captivating of them all, was Triveni's.

She smiled at him, making him weak in the knees.

From the colour on her cheeks it was evident that she was blushing. *Like a bride.*

Prashant's own cheeks turned a deep shade of crimson as Triveni silently mouthed three words to him: 'Happy Valentine's Day.'

Death of a Widower

Monidipa Mondal

(A) WIDOWER had come to live in the second floor flat recently emptied at K-91 Kalsipur Housing Society. His wife had been killed in a bomb blast at a pub two years ago in Bangalore, the unsuspecting victim of a terrorist attack. The news had played in a loop on television. Her name was Hansika Joshi (26), the news tickers said. She was laughing through dimpled cheeks and a ruffianly mop of curls in the photograph that had been on the front page of every newspaper in the country. Her white cotton kurta was printed with orange blossoms. And she was decidedly cute.

Her husband was a software engineer. Vivan Joshi. Everyone knew.

He looked the same way that they remembered him from the newscasts—a little softer around the jaw, a few strands of grey at the temples, but entirely recognizable. He still wore the same kind of starched blue shirt that he had worn on the evening when the TV cameras descended upon him. They remembered his sleeves rolled up to his elbows, on which he had clumsily wiped his eyes as he bawled incoherently at the journalists. He was a small, downcast-looking man, thoroughly ordinary, now, a familiar character in a town where he knew no one.

Every weekday morning at 9.30 he left his flat, climbed down the stairs of K-91 and walked to the bus stand from where he caught a local bus to work. In the evenings, he stayed in. Sometimes there was music from his flat—English rock songs or the soundtrack of a recent Hindi film. While the neighbours could hear the music, it was never loud enough to be considered offensive. Sometimes there were the muffled voices of people on the television. On other evenings there was a profound silence, but the widower always emerged next morning, clean-shaven, neatly dressed and heading for work.

It took Mrs Dasgupta one and a half months to make the acquaintance of the widower—an unusually long time by her estimate, for Mrs Dasgupta collected people with the eagerness and consuming curiosity that some children reserved for stamps or butterflies. Every resident of the K Block was a subject of her interest. But she did not know how to start talking to the reserved widower, until the day at the sabzi mandi when he spoke to her himself.

'Auntyji, namaste,' he had stopped by Mrs Dasgupta, clutching his grocery bag and smiling politely. 'May I ask a question? I have recently moved into this neighbourhood and need some...um...help.'

Mrs Dasgupta was charmed right away. She sized him up and decided he couldn't be older than her own Subhojit, a software engineer himself, now with God's grace settled in San

Francisco with his wife and small son. But this poor boy, the widower, was unfortunate. He looked underweight and pale. Perhaps she could invite him for the occasional dinner with Mr Dasgupta and herself. She returned his smile enthusiastically, 'I know you have, beta—Vivan, isn't it? How have you been getting on?'

Vivan's gaze slipped down to his rubber chappals, but he pushed his smile back up and answered, 'I've been fine. I stay busy with work. Uh, if it is all right, could you tell me how to find a domestic help? I'm afraid it's not always easy with all the housework—'

'Of course, beta, of course,' Mrs Dasgupta happily agreed. 'How can a young man like you look after himself all alone, without a wife, without...' He nodded along weakly.

Mrs Dasgupta clucked her tongue and added, 'But God has his eyes trained on you, beta. He does everything for the best. I mean, she... your wife... was not being quite...umm... faithful to you, no?'

Vivan developed instant rigor mortis.

'Uh, no, I don't think so. I'm quite sure there was nothing like that. Why would you think such a thing?'

'But that man with her when she—?'

The cheeky, ungrateful chap cut her off with a terse: 'He was her friend from college. They had met up for a drink after work. I don't think anything in the news suggested otherwise at any point of time. Please don't make or spread these assumptions. Namaste.'

The drop in temperature hit her like a physical blow. He left in a huff, leaving Mrs Dasgupta to stare at his receding back, angry and dismayed beyond belief. But, of course, everyone knew what she was talking about! The young man who had been drinking with that luckless girl at the pub, while her husband was held up at his office, working all night. The one who had died with her at the same blast. Everyone knew. And such things did happen. All she was trying to say was that she understood.

※

That precisely was the subject of discussion later that afternoon, when Mrs Dasgupta came over for a round of chai-biscuit with Ragini's mother. Ragini and her parents lived in the other flat on the second floor of K-91, right across the landing from the taciturn widower. They had heard or seen very little of him. How could one feel safe with such ill-bred fellows running amok, especially those of us with young daughters at home, Ragini's mother intoned as Mrs Dasgupta finished narrating her experience.

Ragini slipped out of the room when she was sure neither of them would mind, returned to her computer and looked up Hansika Joshi's Facebook profile. After her death her husband hadn't closed down his wife's account but, instead, turned it into a public forum, accepting friend requests from anyone who supported his campaign against terrorist attacks on civilians. Ragini was one of the five thousand names in the friends list. In the wake of the tragedy, she had joined hundreds of others at a candlelight vigil at her college to remember the victims, sitting in silence in front of that laughing portrait of Hansika, her much-maligned college friend and three others, their faces half-hidden behind heavy garlands of jasmine. Some months later, when the ripples of the gruesome episode had ebbed, Ragini had flinched seeing the dead woman's birthday reminder flashing on her Facebook home page. She'd realized that that was the effect intended—to remind everyone that the dead did not go down the recycle machines along with old newspapers.

But despite his online activities, few people had got to know Hansika's husband personally. He did not accept friend requests to his own account; and although he left all of Hansika's photos untouched—once again, as a reminder of the life she had lived, day in and day out—he had untagged himself from them. There were a lot of photos on Hansika's profile. She had been a very attractive woman, with a winsome smile and well-toned body that she liked to dress in various fashions. In their wedding photos she wore a sari of dark green and gold, matched perfectly with her husband's intricate gold sherwani. At their honeymoon in Goa they were both in T-shirts and shorts, grinning and making faces at each other. Ragini's gaze lingered over the photos of the handsome couple. The man in the photos looked radiant and about ten years younger than the phantom presence next door, even though these albums dated back to only four years ago. Vivan's eyes glowed with warmth and tenderness as he gazed at his beautiful wife. He looked almost enviably handsome. Browsing again through the pages on Facebook, Ragini wasn't even sure if it was pity or jealousy that thumped a fist into her heart. The couple seemed to inhabit a bubble of perfection, the sort that was idealized in TV commercials for gadgets and five-star cruises.

Ragini's own life would never be so picturesque. It was almost a year since college had been over, and college, too, in this small town had hardly been as exciting as the films and TV serials had promised in her younger years. No man ever swept her off her feet with a dashing proposition or a bouquet of roses; in fact, none of her male classmates even looked like they could moonlight as any kind of romantic hero. The best of them dressed shabbily, kept to their all-male groups and could hardly look into the eyes of a girl and talk. The ones who did try to talk to girls were another kind of an annoyance—the ruffianly roadside Romeo that no girl of decent upbringing or taste could bear to associate with. Ragini had never spent time alone with a man, never seen the inside of a discotheque, never taken a sip of alcohol or, God forbid, a drag from a cigarette. When her best friend was married off just after their final exams, it had quite succinctly hit home that she was the next victim for the noose.

There did not seem many options to hold off the inevitable. Ragini's parents were not unkind. Had she come to them with a suitable boyfriend or any particular career prospects, they would, perhaps, had let her have her way. But there was nothing so extraordinary. Her life was ordinary through and through. She did nothing much any more except sitting around at home, watching films on her computer, helping her parents around and meeting the occasional prospective groom they brought in for her. She didn't want to marry any of them—older versions of the men from her college, inoffensive and safe but thoroughly unexciting. Ragini had never been a rebel or even especially unhappy with her lot, but sometimes these days, she felt a desperate urge to do something drastic, shock everyone and break away from all this ordinariness that had become her life. If she had to marry, she would rather marry someone who understood her, talked and joked with her and took enviable photos just like that couple on Facebook. She could only be happy with that kind of love—the flawless kind.

But had this couple's love really been as flawless and idealised as it looked? Ragini was often unsure. There was much about this widower character that did not match up. He was a man with the kind of murky values that did not get a dent from his wife drinking at a pub with another man while he stayed back at work; but clearly it had not been an indifferent marriage, not from the way he had whimpered on national television, not from the way he hung on to his campaign for justice and remembrance long after the story had faded from the public memory. Every now and then, he still updated his wife's Facebook account. But, sadly, the rest of him had turned out little else like the man Ragini had expected.

About a week ago, just a little past midnight, the widower had rung the bell at their flat. It was an odd night to come calling—or perhaps a well-planned one, she now wondered—for Ragini's parents were out of station, leaving her alone in the house. He had stared at her with surprise, as if he didn't expect a young woman to answer the door at that hour.

'Sorry to disturb, but may I borrow a matchbox? My supplies have run out.' Glancing at his watch, he had added with an apologetic smile, 'It's late.'

Ragini had asked him to wait, latched the door and fetched a box of matches from the kitchen. The man had thanked her, taken out a packet of Navy Cut from the pocket of his shorts and lit one.

Her eyes widened. 'You smoke?'

'My only vice,' he had smiled, slightly tilting his head.

'Did you smoke when your wife was—?' Ragini blurted before she could stop herself.

'Why, yes.' He had added with a grin, 'When she felt kind, she would even let me borrow from her. But she smoked Milds, usually too bland for my taste.'

It was puzzling. He had updated Hansika's Facebook page two days ago, reminding the world that the Bangalore pub bombers had still not been intercepted, that he was awaiting justice for his dead wife. But there was no trace of that intensity or pain in his demeanour that night. Instead, he was trying to sound...flippant?

Ragini had peered uneasily through the half-open door of his flat behind him. The darkened room was filled with the spectral blue of the frozen TV screen. A half-finished beer mug stood on the low table in front of the sofa.

'Do you...er...drink yourself to sleep every night?'

'Nothing like that!' The widower had chuckled, as if the suggestion was absurd. 'I'm just preparing to watch the game tonight.' He noticed her incomprehensible expression and explained, 'There's a football match. Chelsea against Manchester United.'

'Oh.'

'Thank you, again,' he waved the matchbox at her expressionless face. 'Let me not intrude on you any longer. Goodnight.'

It was only after she had shut and securely bolted the door that Ragini remembered that the man hadn't even asked her her name.

There was something oddly unpleasant about the widower—on this everyone in the housing society agreed. It was as if he was violently spurning the sympathy that was due to him, the sympathy that the small town had gregariously decided to bestow upon him. He stiffened if the billing-counter guy at the supermarket addressed him by the name; made non-committal noises and slipped away with some excuse if the neighbourhood uncles tried to gently engage him in a conversation about his past. Not to mention that the still affronted Mrs Dasgupta never got around to finding him a domestic help.

'I could have asked our Malati only—she was looking for another house to work at,' she explained to Ragini's mother one Sunday evening, flailing her arms like fans, 'but who can guarantee anything about men like that? Who knows anything about what goes on in that house? Has he ever invited anyone in? I may not have a daughter, but these girls are like my daughters only, no?'

Ragini's mother, always the mild-mannered follower in these conversations, dutifully nodded. Sitting at the table with the two older women who never talked directly to her but nonetheless expected her presence, Ragini played absently with the crocheted edge of the tablecloth. *What did the widower really do with his time after he returned from work?* They were next-door neighbours, but two weeks had passed before she had run into him again. This time it had been on the first-floor landing. He was presumably returning early from work since it was only 3 p.m. Their eyes had met and he had smiled, and so had she.

'How was your match?' she asked.

'Hm?'

'Chelsea against Manchester United,' Ragini had said, gingerly plucking the unfamiliar words out of her memory.

'Oh, that one? It was cool. We won!'

'Who are "we"?' said Ragini.

'Chelsea, of course! It's been a while, though. We've won a couple more matches since then, actually—very good place on the League Table right now!' He had suddenly broken into a sharp chuckle. 'You couldn't care less, could you?'

'Well…'

'Then why ask about it?'

'Just something to make conversation,' Ragini had mumbled defensively.

'You don't have to make conversation with me,' the widower had stung back in an instant. 'It's not social service.'

'I didn't know talking to one's next-door neighbour was considered social service.'

For some reason, this softened his next words. 'You're lying, of course, but at least you have the decency to pretend. That's more respect than my dignity has been used to receiving of late.'

'Thank you.'

'Come over sometime, then, Miss Next-Door Neighbour,' he had said, completely ignoring her sarcasm. 'We can make conversation over dinner, hopefully on subjects other than the English Premier League. Or if you like to watch movies, I have quite a good collection.'

'You don't even know my name,' Ragini could not help pointing out.

'But you know mine. You also know my age, where I've come from, where I work, how much I earn, who my psychiatrist is, hell, you probably know my…my…shoe or shirt size,' he had shrugged. 'Besides the greatest tragedy of my life, of course. Does that give you a kind of better understanding of me?'

The brutal words had made Ragini flinch. Each of those minor details had really been reported by the media—well, not quite down to his shoe or shirt size—and he must have come across every one of them, felt intensely that slow degradation into a character in a public drama, the peeling away of what had once been a private life. 'I…I didn't mean it that way. I'm sorry,'

The widower gave her a blast of a glare from behind his glasses. 'Don't bother. I'm sick of people feeling sorry for me.'

Then he had pursed his lips and walked past her, up the staircase and inside his flat, leaving Ragini stranded on the first-floor landing.

For days, she felt inclined to agree with Mrs Dasgupta. There was something crazy about the widower, something irretrievably decayed—a pity for a man so young, so quietly intense, but nothing that could be set right any longer with forthright sympathy or warmth. This man was done, broken, finished, sucked dry. He would never laugh again in a way that made his eyes glow with tenderness and warmth. Ragini realized with some mortification that she had been staring at his photos on Facebook again.

A chat window popped open at the right corner of her screen.

'Hi Ragini (now that I know your name).'

She stared at the chat window. Technically, everyone on her friend list was entitled to chat with her, but this person had been a little beyond the expected.

Ragini typed: 'Hansika. You're dead.'

'You know, it's unhealthy to obsess about dead people.' A smiley cheekily appeared at the end of the sentence.

'You're telling me,' Ragini typed.

Five minutes elapsed before a new message popped up on Ragini's chat window: 'Even the ones you have loved with your life. Especially them. Hold on to them in the ways they've lived;

not in the ways they ceased to live. It's not so complicated, is it? Incredible how many people would have it the other way round.'

'And you say this on chat from a dead woman's account.'

'I say this on chat to a woman who's young and alive, hoping to remind her of the unhealthiness of having "liked" fifty-seven of a dead woman's photos in the past one hour. Thank you, but seriously, stop it. I live next door.'

Ragini blushed furiously at the computer screen.

He added, 'And I am not dead yet, contrary to what everyone would like to believe.' Ragini wondered if he meant himself or his wife in his statement.

Ragini typed furiously: 'I thought you still loved her.' *Why all this pretence, otherwise—constantly updating her status, reminding people, the harrowing raid for justice?*

'I do. I hope I always will. She was one of the best people I've known. She had made my life beautiful.' A smiley appeared, more serene and composed. 'But she is gone. And I've made the choice to celebrate her life with my life, instead of letting her death suck me into mine.'

'Have you always been such a philosopher?' Ragini asked, surprised at the resolution in that thought.

'Philosopher? Ha ha, hardly! Just a regular guy driven into a series of difficult situations. What would you have done?'

Gone insane, I suppose, Ragini bitterly thought. *Committed suicide.*

'Exactly,' he replied, startling her out of her skin.

'I'm sorry,' she quickly typed back.

'Don't be. That makes it worse. What has happened to me will never be undone, but I can still talk about...football. Or movies. None of the reports mentioned this, but I've always been a real movie buff. Nearly went to film school. What are some of your favourites?'

Ragini smiled. 'I really liked *English Vinglish* of late.'

'Oops, haven't watched that one,' he wrote back, 'I rarely go out to watch new films at the halls any more. You know how it is. Maybe I should lose my glasses, or start keeping a beard. You know, try something different from my usual look?'

The imagination made her giggle. 'I have the DVD, if you'd like to watch.'

'Would you like to watch it again?'

'That's what I suggested.'

The smiley reappeared. 'My pleasure.'

'Sometime soon, then?'

'Sometime soon.'

The next time when Ragini sent a friend request to Vivan Joshi on Facebook, he accepted it without protest.

Post-Coital Cigarette

Aarti Venkatraman

I LOVE her so much.

What else can I say? I love her so much. So much. More than oceans and skies and universes and galaxies, and if there is anything beyond that, I love her more than that. I am not kidding. I am *not*.

Damn you. What do *you* know about love?

What do *you* know about wanting someone so much, needing someone so much that you're not alive if you're not with them. You count the minutes till you can see her, when just one smile from her brightens your day, and when every tear she sheds is like steel knives peeling the skin off your body.

What do you know about that, huh? Nothing. Not one damn thing.

Because most of you, punks and jerks and assholes—y'all are afraid to love like that. Cowards. The whole lot of you!

But I am not one of you.

I love. I love deeply, passionately, with every fibre of my being. She's mine, you see. She always has been. And occasionally, when even she forgets that, I just have to remind her again that she is mine. Sometimes, it takes kisses. Sometimes, fists. Whatever the method, whatever the means, I've always known she is mine.

You know something? I believe in all that soulmate crap. Looking at me, you wouldn't believe that because of my formal clothes and the mean machine that I drive—not to mention my loathsome job at the phone company.

But I have friends—men who I shoot the shit with—who'll tell you: Hey, that guy? Man, he believes in soulmates.

He also believes in fate.

He is my fate.

I knew that at age eight. And I know that now; after three years of marriage and all the hell she's put me through. I remember the time when she went missing for three days just because I didn't visit her dad at the hospital, while he was getting operated for his heart. I had work; I was busy, man! She should have understood. Instead, she didn't say a word, just vanished from my life for three days after the old man was back home. That time is branded in my brain. I searched the whole city for her; there was even a story about me in the papers: 'A man screams his wife's name on the roads like a lunatic.'

I am that lunatic. And I love her like one.

Of course, we mated like bunnies when she came waltzing home again after putting me through seventy-two hours of the purest hell. You'd think that would be the time when I'd want to hit her. Use my fists and really go to town on her, so she'd never ever leave me. But right then I was just so grateful, so pitifully grateful that she had come back. That she wasn't dead in a ditch somewhere. That she hadn't really gone somewhere and left me alone, forever. I would have then been doomed to search the whole earth for my bride—just like Dracula. I wasn't Dracula then. I was her husband, just the guy who loved her.

※

Love. Sometimes, she just didn't grasp that concept.

She told me that she'd always known we were going to be together: back when we were next-door neighbours playing 'Chase' on the terrace of our building in Malad. She remembered the time when we were eight and I'd come to her school on the first day and hit this poor snot for talking to her. *My* girl.

We were together during school, college, first jobs—and years later when we married, I would often wonder why she stayed with me. I know why *I* lived with her, even when I hated her for making me need her so much. For making me want to breathe the very air she breathed; when following her seemed like an acceptable thing to do because it meant seeing her, breathing in her alluring scent.

And she, damn her, knew that.

She knew the power she had over me. Even when I hit her, even when I slammed her against the wall that one time, then all those times. She knew. She knew I'd always come back to her. That I'd always crawl back to her just so she'd take me in once again. So I'd know peace again.

Because nothing—nobody else—else gave me peace.

Not booze, or cigarettes or other women. When I screwed another woman and went home to my wife, she knew it. But she never said a word. She would simply look at my reflection in the mirror. Like she was disappointed in me in some way.

Like it was expected. Like she was so goddamn superior to me, that...that ungrateful bitch!

I married her, didn't I? We were just two kids out of college, running up to the Magistrate's Court in Bandra, the minute we got our graduation degrees, eager to start our new life together.

And I supported her when she went to school to study to become an accountant. And all those professors and classmates, all those men—bastards!—looking at her, talking to her, when they knew she was mine. I ask you, what else was I supposed to do, but follow her, curtail her movements? To make her understand that she was mine. Just mine.

All mine.

I remember the first time we ever got drunk. It was her eighteenth birthday and we had taken off in my beat-up Maruti 800, with a whole pitcher of Kingfisher. College was months away and I had all summer with her. She was so beautiful, her lustrous black hair flying as we went down the highway. Her brown eyes laughing at me, and her lips all pink and moist from kissing me. We were drunk when, within half an hour of hitting the highway, I made my move on her. Then she made hers and somehow, my shirt came off and then her top came off and then our jeans came off, and I was inside her. It was awkward and painful for her. She cried—how she cried!—her nails digging into my sweaty skin. I wanted to yell at God for making me hurt her. But I held on. Savouring the moment.

That was the night I watched porn for the first time. Because I wanted to learn how to pleasure her. How to hurt her.

Now, I wait for her so we can do it all over again.

She's late from work, as usual. There is dinner on the table, the morning's leftovers. And I can see the enlarged print of our wedding photo, she in a red sari and me in black formals, occupying pride of place on our living room wall. Two twenty-one-year olds who were so crazy in love that they had to get married. Plus, she was pregnant at the time.

I blink because I can feel that familiar howling grief that consumes me as I think about what might have been. We could have been proud parents by now and posed for happy family pictures. Instead, she comes home late from work and disappears for days on end. Like the time when I was late for a movie show.

It's not fair. I love her, what else am I supposed to do? I know she doesn't want to live with the monster she's created. Yes, she created it even when we were as young as eight.

That monster is love.

I call it Me.

The key turns in. I hastily stub out my cigarette; she hates the smell. See, I do try to keep her happy. But I know I am failing. How can I keep her happy, keep her at all, if she doesn't want to stay with me? If she doesn't love me anymore?

'Hi, jaan,' she calls out as she walks into the bedroom. I am seized with panic and desperation and fear. I can't lose her. How can I live if she leaves?

'Hi, sweetheart,' I say.

She flings her handbag on the bed. 'It was a hell of a day. The clients are crazy, I tell you. Loaded, but crazy. You had dinner?' she smiles at me. The traitorous bitch. Does she really care about my dinner?

'No, jaan,' I reply. 'I was waiting for you so we can have it together.'

She laughs and tucks her hair behind her ear; I can see she is pleased. I want to wind her hair around my hands and feel all that warm, heavy weight in my hands. Then twist and twist and twist, until I hear her neck snap. I blink. A bit too rapidly.

She holds my gaze. 'It's so late, silly. You shouldn't wait for me like that.'

'That's all right, honey. I love you.' I stretch my legs on the bed and continue checking out the India-Pak cricket match score on the laptop.

She shakes her head with a small sigh and goes into the bathroom. I keep the laptop aside and follow her there. When she washes her face the water splashes down the front of her blue shirt. I catch a glimpse of the white bra underneath. I am tempted to rip off her clothes, but I get a grip on myself.

'Do you?' I whisper.

She cocks a brow and proceeds to dry her face with a towel. 'Do I what?' she asks.

'Do you love me?'

She laughs again and hangs the towel on the rack. She doesn't get it, does she? I want to slap her .

She places her hand on my shoulder. 'I am tired, jaan. And hungry. Let's eat, please. Okay?'

She tries to get past me, but I grip her wrist.

'Do you love me?' I ask her evenly.

She blinks at me and gently tries to shake off my grip. 'Of course, I love you. What sort of stupid question is this?' She seems composed enough. Bitch.

'How do I know you love me, huh?' I inch closer to her.

Her face hardens. 'Look, I am going to have dinner. We

can continue this while eating, okay?' She tries again to jerk her hand off but I hold on tighter. Tight enough to bruise it, which is, of course, what she wants all along. She wouldn't annoy me like this if she didn't want it.

'You're hurting me, jaan. Let go of my hand,' she says in a low voice, looking me squarely in the eye.

I let her go, trying to ignore the redness around her wrist. 'Sorry. Let's eat.'

We eat in silence and then clear up as if nothing had transpired moments before. When we are finally in bed, I try to kiss her, but she says, 'No, not tonight, I am so tired.'

'Come on, jaan,' I say.

'I have a presentation tomorrow. Not tonight, please,' she says and turns her back on me. I grab her shoulder and turn her around. She curses under her breath and scratches me. I follow her when she gets up and walks to the bedroom door. I grab her again and press my lips on her mouth and kiss her. To my surprise, she kisses me back with fervour. I push her against the wall, and pull down my shorts. I groan when she bites me on the shoulder. I try to get my fly to open. All along, she moans and mouths loud protests, while her hands tug at my hair. And when I take her standing up, I feel myself going deep inside her—till I am a part of her, and she is a part of me. I know she will never leave me if I keep her like this forever.

'Do you love me?' I ask her in a hoarse voice, for the second time that night.

'Yes, yes. GOD, YES,' she screams. She orgasms and collapses with a shudder in my arms.

Then I slap her and hiss into her ear, 'Then come home on time so we can have dinner early.'

When she knees me hard in the groin, I howl and wrench

away from her. She slides down the wall and I look at her with distaste. I cannot fathom why I still want her. It's not like she is the most beautiful woman, or the sexiest or that she even gives me head. I just love her the only way I know how. I love her like a man loves a woman. Is *that* a crime?

'Go to sleep now,' she spits at me as she curls up on the floor like a wilted flower.

Suddenly, I am overcome with guilt and feel like an asshole.

I venture near her, and she slaps me hand away. I touch her cheek, now a pale purple. She slaps my hand again.

'Sorry,' I mumble and run my fingers through my hair. *God, what have I done?*

When I caress her cheek, she starts crying.

'Why do you do this to me?' she beseeches me with her limpid eyes.

I shake my head. *I don't know.*

I gather her in my arms and carry her to our bed. And then we make love; this time slowly, passionately, like it was a never-ending night.

And when it's finally over, in a resounding climax, she kisses my hand and says in a tired voice, 'I love you. I don't want to prove it, but I do love you.' My heart bursts inside my chest and I gather her close, and wish there was some way I could never let her go. Or hurt her.

'I love you too,' I whisper in her hair as her eyelids start drooping.

I toss from side to side, fighting sleep. I look at my wife's sleeping profile.

Why do you do this to me? she seems to ask.

I fumble for an answer. So you'll never leave me? Because you're better than me and you have no reason to love me?

Because you're good and kind and nice, and I am not? Because I am twisted and messed up, and loving you is just not enough? I stare at the ceiling for a while. Yes, it's not enough.

I love her, but I don't know what to do to show her the extent of my feelings.

I look at our bedroom, illuminated by the street light. The blue and yellow floral bedspread that we'd picked at HomeStop, the olive green curtains. The colours of the walls are a pale fuchsia pink that she'd made me mix about four times before I got the shade right. There is all her stuff on the dressing table, and my glasses, next to her watch, on the nightstand. This, I realize with a start, is my whole life.

And I can't have her out of it.

I know of only one way to ensure this never happens. That she never leaves me.

It's surprisingly easy—leaving the gas stove on, pouring kerosene over everything: the curtains, the bed sheets, and the bed itself. And then the wooden dressing table with the matching pouffes. For a foolproof plan I lay a trail of kerosene right down the living room, and then I splash some on the room's curtains as well.

Feeling calmer, I get back into bed with her. She is sleeping serenely.

'I love you so much,' I whisper in her ear. I light my cigarette, feeling at peace finally. The deed is done. We'll be together forever. And she won't ever leave me—because she can't. I bite back a smile. We'll be together forever in death.

I inhale and exhale, do smoke rings. She wrinkles her nose in sleep, because she really detests cigarettes.

'I am quitting tomorrow, jaan,' I tell her.

I am down to the last quarter inch of my Marlboro, and I

toss the smouldering stick on the bed. Right between us. Then I start lighting the matches and throwing them down.

I lie back down and watch the flames climb the bed. I hold her close and an intense feeling hits me in my gut. I love her and this is what I am supposed to do.

Fire. It's such a beautiful thing, such a cleansing thing. It catches and never lets go. It swallows you and consumes you whole. You're lost in it and burning in its tongue. Your skin and your organs, and your nails and your hair. The smell is awful and acrid and you want to throw up, but you can't. Because your throat and your teeth are burning, too.

God, the clean, *clean* release of our combined suffering. Setting our house and ourselves on fire—it would be so easy, such a definitive thing to do.

I hold her close and shake off the unruly images in my head, of burning ourselves and our apartment. The images are so real that I can almost feel the flames licking my face.

I pick up my Marlboro pack from the side table and give it a long hard look. The images of our corrosive bodies refuse to budge from my mind. Should I try it?

Yes, I can do it, I decide. I can, but not tonight.

I reach for my lighter, flick it open, and light my cigarette. I look at my sleeping wife whom I love so much. So very much.

Siddharth

Pooja Pillai

*T*HERE WAS a time when I wanted to look as lovely as Andrea Corr. I listened to a lot of music back then and attached different fantasies to each song that I heard. For instance, when I played 'Runaway', I would imagine Siddharth and me, hand in hand, going somewhere far away, as Sharon Corr's violin played in the background and Andrea voiced our inarticulate passion. In those dreams, I always looked like Andrea and Siddharth, strangely, looked exactly like himself. Of course, it didn't strike me as being peculiar then. I was fifteen and Siddharth was perfect to me.

One evening, I called him up, ostensibly to ask him about the next day's homework. 'So, what have you been listening to lately?'

There was the slightest pause before he replied, 'I only listen to the golden oldies, you know. '90s music is such a sell-out. I'm telling you, none of this is going to last into the next decade.'

Fortunately, he didn't ask me what *I* had been listening to. He might have flipped if I had said The Corrs.

'So what is your favourite band?' I asked him.

'The Beatles,' he said, without missing a beat. 'Only they made real music.'

The next day, I surprised my dad by asking him to play *Revolver* as he drove me to school. He had the coolest collection of old pop songs and had tried many times to educate me on those tracks.

He cocked an eyebrow. 'I thought you didn't like the Beatles.'

'Only they made real music, you know.' I said primly and looked straight ahead at the road.

Until then, the only time I had actually listened to anything by the Beatles had been during a free period when our teacher asked us all to perform something. The class sat with polite patience through my rendition of *Marugelara O Raghava*, my favourite Carnatic composition. I was learning advanced Carnatic vocal music and used every opportunity I got to practice the ragas.

Others got a more enthusiastic response. Teena did some Bharatanatyam, and all the boys fell in love with her—at least those who hadn't already done so. She was our class beauty; tall, lissome with limpid dancer's eyes. The class joker, Nimit, mimicked many of us and our teachers, and nearly brought the house down. Some others sang Hindi film songs, two others recited poetry, one sang a haunting ghazal and one a Krishna bhajan.

Of course, it was Siddharth who sang the only English song of the afternoon—*Help!* by the Beatles. It was quite the scandale du jour when he announced the name of his item and everyone talked about how Siddharth was 'showing off' by singing an English song.

'He's not been the same since he spent the summer holidays in the US,' Ankita whispered into my ears. 'Now he thinks he is better than us.' I had never seen her roll her eyes like that.

The real joke, however, was that Siddharth sang very badly. He thought he was doing a mighty fine job of it, though. But as I listened to the low thrum in the classroom, generated by the suppressed giggles of my classmates, I felt embarrassed for him. Teena delicately held her handkerchief to her mouth and Nimit looked like he had hit the mother lode. My collar felt tight and hot and I didn't want to look at Siddharth. Not because I thought I would laugh, but because my dismay would show so clearly.

But of course, Siddharth was blissfully unaware that he was becoming the laughing stock of the class and that even if no one ever dared say anything to his face, his classmates would spend the next few weeks making fun of him behind his back.

Siddharth wouldn't have bothered himself about it, even if he had realized how terribly he sang. I think that's why I fell in love with him so madly, badly and deeply. He was the rebel who spoke his mind and refused to listen to anything the teachers said, without lobbing a few questions at them. When all the other boys of our class thought it was cool to listen to Metallica, he announced that hip hop was the real thing. And when the rest moved on to hip hop, he went right back to loving Metallica. His hair always stood up straight and unoiled and his pants were always trendily baggy at the knees. He was also the only person in our class—boy or girl—who refused to wear contact lenses. Right till the time of our graduation from school, he wore thick-framed glasses that gave him an owlish look. He didn't care, and neither did I.

'Doesn't it ever bother you that the attendance register lists all the boys first and then the girls?' he asked me once when we were coming out of the school canteen.

I had never thought of it that way. I thought only girls noticed such things.

'If I had been one of you girls, I would have said something about it by now,' he continued in an even tone, but took agitated steps to our class.

All I could do was look away sheepishly, my latent feminism now stirred.

Soon it was time to face our Board exams and bid adieu to school. One of our richer classmates, Noel, was throwing a 'Last Day of School' party on the spacious lawns of his Jayanagar house and we were all having as grand a time as we could. Acutely aware that we wouldn't all be meeting again, as usual, the next day and all the days to follow, was a sad thought, but we bore it well. We had stuffed ourselves with fine food, danced a lot and were engaged in a childish game of 'Catch', when the most thrilling moment of my life happened.

I don't remember whose idea it had been to play 'Catch'. Someone suggested it, everyone else agreed that it would be fun to play it 'one last time' before we all grew up. And then we were dashing about madly, trying to catch each other in Noel's lawns.

It was as I paused to catch my breath that Siddharth came and took my hand. I was surprised and insanely thrilled that he would do so in front of all our classmates. But to my dismay, no one was looking. Before I could react, Siddharth quickly hurried me toward one of the open doors of the house, into a long dark corridor. My breath had quickened. I knew something momentous was about to happen. I could feel it in my bones. Perhaps I would experience the first kiss that I had dreamed of for so long?

Siddharth cupped my face in his hands. 'I'll miss you,' he said.

'I'll miss you too,' I whispered back. When I had imagined this scene a hundred times before, I had thought I would cry and he would hold me and then kiss me reassuringly. I knew no better for I had been raised on a staple diet of Bollywood movies. Instead, when the momentous act occurred, I was dry-eyed and surprisingly lucid.

Siddharth was dry-eyed, too. He didn't look a wee bit embarrassed and he didn't shuffle his feet. Instead, he continued to look at me from behind his owlish glasses. Then, reaching into his pocket, he brought out a small box with a little blue ribbon on top.

'Please take this, Janki. I wanted to get you something better, but after I bought the Limp Bizkit cassette, I had very little money left. I suppose I should have waited till next month's allowance, but I thought it would be right to give you something on our last day together.' I couldn't reply. At that moment, weirdly enough, it occurred to me that I wouldn't even feel this way for Brad Pitt.

I took the box and opened it. Inside, was a pair of earrings shaped like kittens. As I gingerly ran a finger over them, I finally felt tears prickling at my eyelids. Perhaps it were the words 'our last day together' that did it. In any case, I suddenly felt childish and stupid. I hadn't got Siddharth anything. It hadn't even occurred to me. I told him so in an apologetic tone.

'Hey, that's cool,' he waved aside my stumbling words, 'It's not a big deal. Just something, you know. Because I will miss you, Janki. You will write to me, won't you?' He had always talked about wanting to go to college in the US, but it was at this moment that I really understood what that would mean.

It would mean that we wouldn't be able to talk as frequently as we did now.

Yes, yes, a hundred times yes, I wanted to say. Instead, I said, 'I will write to you, of course. I just wish we could talk on the phone. I will miss you too…so much.' I heard my voice quiver. Oh, God, no, I didn't want to burst into tears now.

We stood like that for a few minutes, preferring silence over words.

'Janki…' Siddharth's voice was hoarse when he finally spoke. He reached out and took my hand. I waited, not daring to look him in the eye.

'Janki, I think I really like you. You're…you're special, you know?' He was whispering now. Slowly, he stepped forward and paused. We stood there, hand in hand, him looking at me, me looking at the floor. We were both waiting for the other to make the next move, and we waited a few seconds too long. A sudden cool breeze blew down the corridor and I shivered. It was one of those cold March nights, when a sudden cool breeze can make you wish it was summer. Noel's was one of those long, spread out houses which manage to be massive even without a second storey. With its numerous long corridors and large windows, it was an airy house which could get very cold in the winter months. I had been here for Noel's Christmas parties more than a few times, but it had never seemed chillier to me than it did at that moment.

'Are you feeling cold?' Siddharth asked with concern.

I nodded.

'Here, take my jacket,' he draped his brown leather jacket around my shoulders.

When we emerged on to the lawn a minute later, we found that our classmates had been looking for us. One look at the jacket that had moved from Siddharth's shoulders to mine, and they all acted like their questions had been answered. Ankita later asked me, rather eagerly, if we had finally kissed, to which I should have rather primly declined an answer. Instead, I said 'no', and left to get a Coke.

Siddharth and I didn't see each other much again after the party. The Board exams were upon us soon, then I went off to Kerala for a family wedding and by the time I got back, our results were out. I was eligible for admission to a number of colleges in Delhi University, and I quickly got busy with filling up forms and then flying down to Delhi for the admissions. Siddharth's admission to the University of Pennsylvania had come through a month or two before the Board results were announced. He had already left to spend some vacation time with his extended family in the States, before his semester started over there.

Siddharth's fascination with America was already well-known in our class. That first vacation he had had in the US had convinced him that he was born to live there. 'I might as well start as soon as possible,' he'd told, before he left.

Nevertheless, Siddharth and I managed to stay in touch. Initially, there were a lot of long, detailed emails, but as our respective workloads got heavier, we found it easier to simply chat whenever we bumped into each other online. We never scheduled these chats; I don't know about him, but I often lurked online, just waiting for him to logon. I would then hold off for a decent five minutes before I sent him a message. On some days, I would wait for him to open the conversation, although that was not a uniformly successful strategy. Sometimes he was too busy to chat, and sometimes he never responded. But there were days when he would message back and we would have one of our long meandering conversations. Such sessions would be few and far between and I would often wonder if he had met someone there who would push all his memories of me out of his mind. Such thoughts would make me feel like my heart had dropped through my stomach on to the floor. But each time we did finally talk, I knew that for him, it was still just me.

In the second year of college, we both got mobile phones and took to texting each other at all hours. Sometimes, he would drunk-text me. 'I'm drunk and I can't stop thinking of you' or 'You're the only one I think of.' Even in his inebriated state, he never made a spelling error or used texting abbreviations.

But he never drunk-dialled my number to talk to me. In a way, I suppose I was relieved by that. I wouldn't have known what to say to him. I was always overwhelmed by his declarations of love, or whatever they were, and as usual, when I was overwhelmed, I was tongue-tied.

It was in the third year of college that the texts became infrequent. Slowly, they stopped. I assumed Siddharth had become really busy, because I certainly was and there were days when I didn't even have the time to think about him.

Nevertheless, it was a relief when he called me during the Christmas holidays. We were both in our home town, Bangalore, for a few days and he asked me if we could meet. I agreed in a heartbeat.

'Great, come over to my place tomorrow,' he said.

So the next day, I went dressed in my best sweater and jeans, and wearing brightly coloured socks with my new branded leather sandals. I was feeling better than I had in a long time. I was finally going to meet Siddharth after almost three years, and I was looking my best. I had recently got my hair cut short, and I felt that it highlighted my cheekbones. In my vainer moments, I thought I looked a bit like the model Indrani Dasgupta.

Siddharth was alone at home, reading, and welcomed me with a hot chocolate. He looked the same as ever—those owlish glasses, the wide grin and the unruly mop of hair. The only difference was that he had put on a little weight, but I thought it suited him. He had verged on the skeletal back in school.

'So, how long since you have been back from Delhi?' he asked. There was a slight nasal twang in his voice which hadn't been there before, and which I hadn't noticed when he had called me.

'I arrived about a week ago,' I told him. 'I had no idea you were going to be here.'

I hoped I didn't sound too accusing. After all, strictly speaking, he wasn't my boyfriend, although he had given every indication that he wanted that position.

'Yeah, sorry about that. Work has been piling up and this year has been so busy,' he said.

'Sure,' I said. 'So, when did you arrive from the States?'

'Last Monday, actually,' he said, not a trace of shame in his voice as I sat there, wounded. He had been back in the country for more than a week and had only bothered to call me the day before!

'So, what have you been reading?' I asked, not because I really wanted to know, but because I felt I needed to tide over the moment with some casual conversation. I couldn't imagine what had changed. *I* hadn't changed, I knew that, and my feelings certainly hadn't. I still thought of Siddharth, if not every day, then certainly every other day. I waited for his text messages and I lurked online just to see the indicator next to his name turn green.

'This new book called *The Da Vinci Code*,' he replied.

'What's it like?'

'Well, it's a thriller. Loads of history and religion. Pretty interesting.'

'Hmm...' The words, that once flowed so easily online, were now stuck in my throat.

There was a pause. It was painfully obvious that we were both looking for something to say to each other. Something was clearly wrong, but I couldn't understand why. I was so afraid my bewilderment would show on my face that I was willing to talk about the weather, if it meant that my face would be unreadable. Luckily, he spoke up first.

'What have you been reading?' he asked me.

'Some plays, actually. I just read *Rhinoceros* by Eugène Ionesco.' I threw out the information in an offhand manner, hoping that the obscurity of the name would impress him and make him regret not calling or texting me more often.

He shook his head vehemently. 'Never heard of him.'

'Oh, he's an absurdist. Rather like Samuel Beckett. You've heard of him, I suppose?'

Siddharth's face brightened. 'Oh yes, my girlfriend has Beckett in one of her courses and talks about him often. He wrote something called *Waiting for God*, right?'

'Godot,' I corrected him, feeling the bile rise to my throat. So his reason for wanting to meet me was finally out. Suddenly, Siddharth seemed miles away from me.

He snapped his fingers. 'Yes, Godot. That's the one. I think he's what is known as an 'absurdist', right?'

'Right. Not that I understand what that really means,' I

replied dryly, dropping all my affectations. There was no point to it anymore.

We sat in silence in his living room, submerged in our own thoughts, waiting for the next bright conversation topic to make its appearance.

'Listened to anything new, lately?' he finally asked.

'I don't have time for music anymore.' I had come prepared with some Wikipedia facts on the Beatles, but they had already escaped my mind.

'Oh.'

I couldn't sit in that room, in that loud silence anymore. 'Want to go for a walk?' I asked.

He looked surprised for maybe a moment, but agreed without any protests.

I waited outside in his porch, while he went to his room to change out of his shorts into his jeans and sneakers. The silence had accompanied me outside and was filling up my ears, and I thought I would have to scream to break it. Before I could do anything like that, Siddharth came out. He was holding two bananas.

'Want one?' he asked me.

'Not now,' I said, 'Did you know banana is full of potassium. It's a natural painkiller.'

'Really?'

'Yeah, now you know what to eat when you have a headache.'

It was a wasted joke, for neither of us even smiled.

We turned the corner outside his house and walked on in silence. He broke it to ask about Ankita and Teena and Nimit and the rest, and then there was silence again.

We were close to the housing colony's main gate when I

looked at my watch. 'Listen, it's getting late. I think I should leave now. I don't want to take the bus after dark.'

'Sure. I'll wait with you at the bus stand,' he said.

There was just one other person at the stand, an old lady. I sat down at one end of the bench and Siddharth stood next to me. I looked down at my feet and noticed that my socks were hanging over the edge of my sandals and were quite brown and dirty. Suddenly, I was very angry with myself for wearing socks with sandals. Any sensible person would have worn sneakers, but no sirree, I had wanted to wear my new sandals and, look, now my socks were dirty.

'It's here,' Siddharth told me.

I flagged down the bus and as it stopped, I leaped for the door. I couldn't say with any certainty that Siddharth would hug me goodbye, but I didn't want him to. Not after what he had told me. I waved to him from the foothold and he stood there, waving back, in his jeans that bagged at the knees and hair that stood up straight.

This story won the third prize in the Rupa Romance Contest.

Author Bios

Aurodeep Nandi, 27, currently cycles to work as the Senior Economic Adviser to the British High Commission in New Delhi, after having gained a good deal of weight at the Delhi School of Economics and the London School of Economics and Political Science as a student. Getting sentimental on Rabindra Sangeet and running amok in a tennis court are his top choices for stress busting. Romance, he says, is bit like an iceberg—that simple kiss or a hug, so often conceals a huge infrastructure of moments, stories and emotions.

After being an English tutor for The Refugee Council, Sheffield, UK; an English and Soft Skills Trainer at inlingua, among other things, **Rhiti Bose** is now a mother, a writer and a blogger. She believes in simplicity, love and kindness. Romance, she says, is the oxygen that every couple needs to keep their love alive.

Cecile Rischmann is a linguist, travelling around the world with her gorgeous French expatriate husband, learning new cultures, languages and dance. Romance, she says, is vital to staying alive.

✢

Debosmita Nandy, a lawyer, loves travelling and blogging at debosmita.wordpress.com. She has written for the Chicken Soup series, *The Telegraph* and *The Statesman,* and authored two books on law. A true Kolkata Bong, she now lives in Gurgaon with her husband. Romance, according to her, is knowing the unspoken words, understanding the unexpressed feelings and fulfilling the unstated desires of the person one loves.

✢

Tarunima Mago is an engineer and a management student who can be found reading *Calvin and Hobbes* in class, writing poetry on her blog, dabbling in discussions on finance and biotechnology, and simultaneously, dreaming to be a writer. Romance, she says, is in the unspoken words. It is to embrace another soul without any inhibitions.

✢

Shoma Chakraborty, a Delhiite by birth, loves to work with words. She is a Learning and Development professional by day and a passionate writer in her spare time. She is an avid blogger and a keen observer of life. For her, romance is a never-ending adventure and a beautiful dance of emotions and wills.

✢

Aabhishek Patwari hails from Hyderabad and is now based in Mumbai. After completing his legal education from Pune, he went on to obtain a master's in reputation management from the UK. He has worked with various films and television shows, advising on promotions, scripts and copyrights. Romance, he opines, is elusive—hiding in places you often look at, but never see.

Ad copywriter-turned-journalist, **Sheila Kumar** is the author of *Kith and Kin* (Rupa Publications), a collection of short stories. She calls Bangalore home. Regarding romance, she firmly believes in the power of the moon in June, the heady scent of red roses and TDH men.

A maths graduate from the University of Pune, **Abhishek Mukherjee** is a finance professional. He is an ardent fan of literary classics and believes there is hidden magic in the written word. According to him, love is the ultimate truth of life and romance is the most natural expression of human emotions.

Anita Sarkar has over three decades of experience in advertising and communications. She loves writing and is fascinated by human behaviour. When you are in love, both the ecstasy and the pain are pleasurable, she says.

Meera Rajagopalan is a Chennai-based writer who has worked variously as a journalist, editor and instructional designer in India and the US. She is currently with an NGO that works in rural education. Life interests her and death intrigues her. Love, according to her, is a hydrophobe taking the plunge.

✤

Sudha Subramanian is an independent freelance writer. She writes regularly in various magazines and newspapers in India, the Middle East and the US. She currently lives in Dubai with her family. According to her, romance is a rainbow of emotions that colours everyone's lives with different hues.

✤

Dr Roshan Radhakrishnan, an anaesthesiologist, believes in the healing power of love and laughter, but practices medicine just to be on the safe side. A foodie, animal lover and sitcom addict, he blogs at www.godyears.net. For him, love is when you would do anything to bring a smile on her face and make her feel cherished—expecting nothing in return.

✤

Monidipa Mondal usually drifts through life and is currently cooling her heels in Stirling, Scotland. She has a cat but it's on a different continent. The best romance, she opines, is perhaps the one that overreaches our limitations and brings us the closest we can be to perfection.

✤

Aarti Venkataraman, 27, lives and writes in Mumbai, but hopes of traversing the world for inspiration. Romance, according to her, doesn't always mean happily ever after. Sometimes, the shades are darker and more twisted, and therefore, more fun to explore.

Pooja Pillai is a Mumbai-based journalist and, like most of her tribe, is 'currently working on a novel'. She's the mother of six first drafts and is a slave to Candy Crush, Facebook and potato chips. To her, romance means all the little unexpected interruptions that have the potential to sweeten everyday life or add a dash of mystery to it.